MW01491412

MAC

DURHAM PRIVATE SECURITY
BOOK 1

MELANIE D. SNITKER

DALLIANCE MEDIA, LLC

Mac
Durham Private Security: Book 1
By Melanie D. Snitker

All rights reserved
© 2025 Melanie D. Snitker

Dallionz Media, LLC
P.O. Box 5283
Abilene, TX 79608

Cover Art: Dallionz Media, LLC

Edited by Erynn Newman
www.alittleredink.com

All rights reserved. No part of this publication may be reproduced, distributed, or transmitted in any form or by any means, including photocopying, recording, or other electronic or mechanical methods, without the prior written permission of the author, except in the case of brief quotations embodied in critical reviews and certain other noncommercial uses permitted by copyright law.

Please only purchase authorized editions.

For permission requests, please contact the author at the email below or through her website.

Melanie D. Snitker
melanie@melaniedsnitker.com
www.melaniedsnitker.com

This is a work of fiction. Names, characters, businesses, places, events, and incidents either are the products of the author's imagination or used in a fictitious manner. Any resemblance to actual persons, living or dead, or actual events is purely coincidental.

For Amanda Knox,
my dearest friend
and sister of my heart

ONE

With a grin that made her cheeks ache, Sedona Reeves exited the stage with her guitar in her hands and a bounce in her step. They'd just finished a performance in front of their largest audience to date, and she had a feeling she'd be floating for a long time.

The applause, whistles, and screams of appreciation followed her backstage along with the members of the band. Sedona knew full well she wouldn't be where she was today, experiencing this dream come true, if it weren't for them.

"Can you believe this?" Chloe, Sedona's friend who played the keyboard and piano, practically squealed.

The women hugged as Joel joined them, followed by Nick and Lou. They were all a team and relied on each other, but for Sedona, it was special to be able to see this success with Chloe and Joel. After all, they were the original three back when it all began.

They'd just finished week four of a six-week tour. They'd started in Arkansas, traveled through Oklahoma, and were now in Destiny, Texas. It seemed fitting that the most successful concert so far was in her home state.

That's why she wanted to tour Texas for the final two weeks. With Thanksgiving behind them and Christmas ahead, the timing was perfect. Their last performance would be in Dallas, where she lived. She would stay and enjoy some well-earned time off before starting work on the next project after the new year.

The audience was still applauding, but there was no time for an encore. Sedona was opening for a much larger band, and they'd been told to clear the stage as soon as their set was finished.

That was okay, though. For the first time in a long time, Sedona could see a future where *she* might be that featured artist. Just the idea of it sent another wave of adrenaline through her system. The last ten years hadn't been easy, and her decision to walk away from a label and branch out on her own as an independent artist had been stressful and a lot of work. She'd certainly discovered who her true friends were in the process. Maybe, finally, things would start getting a little easier.

"All right, people." Lou clapped his hands loudly as he often did when he was trying to get everyone's attention. "Let's get our gear and load up. We've got a schedule to keep."

Lou was their band manager and handled all of their sound and technical equipment. While the tone of his voice suggested he was serious, there was a ghost of a smile on his lips. He was enjoying the success tonight as much as the rest of them.

Still, he was right. They needed to get everything loaded up so they could drive the van and trailer to a nearby hotel where they'd be staying tonight and after their next show tomorrow night. The day after that, they'd leave Destiny for Austin.

Although right now, Sedona couldn't fathom being able to

relax long enough to sleep. No, they'd be celebrating with a late meal and plenty of laughter before any of them crashed for the night.

They worked together to pack up their gear. Lou, Nick, and Joel started hauling it from backstage to the cargo trailer, where it would be stored until their next concert.

The thought of the van and trailer brought warmth to Sedona's heart. Her sweet grandmother had insisted on buying both for Sedona when she'd first announced the tour. It was a hugely extravagant gift, and Sedona had originally refused. But Grandma, in her sweet way, reminded her that music was her calling, and that making sure Sedona had a safe way to get between venues would make her grandmother's "old heart happy."

Not only had the van and trailer been a huge blessing over the last four weeks, but they were a gentle reminder that she had someone who supported her and prayed for her.

"I'm starving," Chloe announced as she shouldered a large bag and picked up another.

"Me, too." Sedona picked up her guitar case. "What sounds good? I think we should celebrate."

Chloe nodded, a happy smile on her face as she exited backstage.

Sedona was about to follow when someone stepped up beside her. She looked over and up at Connor Pascal. He'd been hired partway through the tour to accompany them. Though it wasn't his fault, his presence put a damper on the after-concert euphoria.

His being there was a reminder that she'd been receiving distressing letters and other warnings from a potential stalker since they'd left Arkansas. She hoped and prayed that, now that they'd returned to Texas, they'd left her stalker behind.

"Are you ready?" Connor asked, giving her a look of appraisal.

The man was in his early forties. His hair, which was gray at the edges, was cut short. He approached every situation with the same matter-of-fact demeanor, and seeing as her parents had paid for his services and insisted that he accompany them, she had no doubt he was reporting everything back to them—a fact that irked her, seeing as they hadn't been happy about her tour in the first place. In fact, their tour had been fraught with one issue after another. Most of it could be chalked up to coincidence. Bad luck. But there was no ignoring the notes her stalker had been leaving her with details proving he'd personally been to her concerts in Oklahoma.

It was her first tour as an indie artist, but her parents had insisted that their frequent challenges were a strong sign that she shouldn't have gone indie in the first place.

Connor waited patiently for her response.

"Yeah, I'm ready."

With a short nod, he preceded her to the back door that would lead them into the parking lot. "You should know, there's a crowd waiting. Stay close to me, and I'll have you to the van in no time."

A crowd? Waiting for a chance to see or interact with members of the main event's concert, no doubt.

Sedona wasn't prepared for the large group of thirty or more people to see her and immediately move in her direction.

"What's it like to be back in Texas again?"

"Do you regret leaving your label?"

"Sedona! Could you sign this CD for me?"

The album and a permanent marker were placed in her hands before she had a chance to answer.

The idea that someone would want her autograph still surprised her. Connor had her by the elbow, urging her forward, but she stopped anyway and smiled at the teenage girl standing in front of her.

"What's your name?"

"Amy." The girl grinned. The braces on her teeth had purple bands that matched her shirt. "Thank you so much!"

"Of course " Sedona wrote *To Amy* on the CD and then signed it before handing it and the pen back. "Thank you for listening."

Amy held onto the corners to avoid smearing the ink until it dried. "I love your music. I was so excited when I found out you were going to be singing here."

"Can you sign mine, too? Please?"

Sedona sensed Connor's impatience and disapproval as she took the time to sign several more CDs. By that time, she knew she'd postponed their return to the van for as long as she could. "I'm afraid I need to go. But thank you all again for coming to see the show!" She waved at the crowd as Connor, once again, tried to steer her away by the elbow.

Yes, he'd been hired to keep Sedona and the band safe, but his constant need to keep a hand on her while escorting irritated her. She resisted the urge to take a sidestep away from him as the crowd continued to follow them.

Someone shoved an envelope into her hands and nearly tripped her in the process. Connor caught her stumble. "You okay?"

Sedona tried to see who'd given her the envelope, but the crowd moved back toward the venue. Most likely, they'd all gone back inside so they wouldn't miss the next part of the concert. It didn't help that it was already dark, and the parking lot lights cast harsh shadows on everything.

"What is it?" Connor stepped closer, instantly on alert.

There was nothing printed on the outside of the envelope. Still, something about it made her stomach churn. She gave her head a sharp shake. "Let's go."

Now, Connor was the one who had to keep up with her as she crossed the parking lot to where the van waited. A streetlight nearby cast a muted glow over everything.

Sedona stepped up into the van, grabbed her spot in the second row, and released a breath. Joel glanced at her and stopped, his brows drawing together in concern.

"What happened?"

Unable to find the words, she simply held the envelope up.

Connor reached out a hand, and she handed the envelope over. Still outside the van with the sliding door open, he took the envelope, lifted the unsealed flap, and carefully pulled out a piece of cardstock. His frown deepened. "It's another one. Are you sure you want to see it?"

Hands shaking, she took the paper from him and read the words typed on it. "I've watched you from the shadows, and you've never once glanced my way. That's going to change. There's nowhere you can go that I won't find you."

Her fingers suddenly went numb, and the paper fluttered to the floor of the van.

Their voices of concern joined into an indiscernible buzz as Sedona tried to calm her racing heart.

Joel reached down to retrieve the paper and handed it back to Connor.

Sedona wanted to say that this meant nothing. That it was no different from the other notes she'd gotten over the last couple of weeks.

Except she knew that wasn't true.

She brought the seat belt over her shoulder and buckled it. Suddenly cold, she crossed her arms in front of her to keep away a shiver.

Nick, who drove the van, turned the heat up. The cool air in the van was replaced with welcome warmth as the note was passed around the van.

Joel moved to the third row where he usually sat, leaving room for Chloe to take her seat near Sedona. Chloe reached over and gave Sedona a fierce hug before putting her seat belt on.

"I was really hoping we were going to leave this guy behind in Oklahoma."

"Me, too." That's what had kept Sedona looking forward, even when the creepy notes started coming in. She'd convinced herself it was a fan who was following her around in Oklahoma, and once that part of their tour was over, he'd leave her alone.

Connor closed the sliding door and got into the passenger seat up front.

The van got overwhelmingly loud as everyone began weighing in on the possibilities and options.

"This is completely unacceptable," Joel growled.

"No offense to Connor," Chloe cut a look at him, "but I think you should consider hiring someone else to help with security. It wouldn't hurt to have one person watching the van and another accompanying you during performances. I mean, it was creepy before, but this almost sounds like a threat. That brings it to a whole different level."

Connor twisted further in his seat. "I don't think hiring another person is necessary. But if you insist, I'm sure Mr. and Mrs. Reeves would happily send someone down."

That's exactly what Sedona didn't want. She didn't like the idea of having Connor on board as it was, relaying everything to her parents. No doubt they'd hear about this incident before the end of the hour.

Her saving grace was the fact they used a security company in Houston, where they lived, and would insist on sending someone else from there as well. She would use that delay in getting extra help to her advantage.

"No." The word came out forceful. Definitive. Sedona didn't want her parents getting any more involved than they already were.

Good.

"I think hiring someone else is a good idea, but I'm going to look for a company here in town that can start tonight."

The idea that her stalker was out there, possibly watching the van right now, made her more than a little uncomfortable. If he was willing to follow her from Oklahoma to Texas and then risk approaching her in a crowd, she didn't want to think about what else he might be capable of.

TWO

I t wasn't hard to navigate the streets of Destiny, Texas after nine in the evening. Since it was the first week of December, it'd been dark for several hours now, too, encouraging people to stay home unless they had somewhere else they needed to be. Mac Durham checked the side mirror and changed lanes.

"According to this, Sedona Reeves released her first single ten years ago." Mac's half-brother, Cole, sat in the passenger seat and continued reading from his phone. "She released singles until one song went viral for being used on social media about five years ago, and she was snatched up by a major label. She saw quite a bit of success for several years until she dropped the label over some kind of dispute last year. From the look of things, she's been struggling until the current tour, which has been shining some light on her indie album."

"Are there any indications online about her stalker?" It wasn't entirely unusual to have a potential client contact them about a job with an immediate start. Mac was surprised, however, to be asked to go out to meet her so late in the evening. All Miss Reeves had told Livi over the phone was that she was having trouble with a stalker and needed to hire someone to accompany her for the rest of her tour.

Livi, their sister and the youngest in the family, had trouble containing her excitement. Apparently, she'd listened to Miss Reeves' music for several years now. She likely would've asked to accompany Mac to this introductory meeting instead of Cole if she hadn't promised to help their mom with something tonight.

A smile tugged at the corners of Mac's mouth. He might have to see if he could get an autographed CD to take back to her before it was all over.

He glanced at Cole. "Can you find a tour schedule? See what we're looking at?"

Cole searched for a moment and then read the dates out loud.

So, they'd still be in Destiny through tomorrow evening, at least. That was good. It'd give them a chance to speak to Miss Reeves and put together some kind of plan before she and her crew left town.

A well-lit hotel sign rose high above the road ahead, letting them know they were close. Once in the parking lot, he found a spot near the main entrance.

Mac parked his black Ford Explorer and got out. The slam of his door was echoed by Cole's. Inside the hotel, an employee stood behind the main counter and greeted them with a friendly wave.

A man approached them from the other side of the lobby. "Are you from Durham Private Security?"

"That's us. I'm Mac Durham, and this is Cole Shepherd." He stretched out his hand.

The other man seemed to be sizing them up as he shook their hands. "Connor Pascal. Security for Sedona Reeves." There was no smile, although he didn't appear entirely unfriendly. "If you'll follow me."

He led them into a lounge area off the lobby where three men and two women sat scattered amongst the tables and chairs. One woman stood and approached, her honey blonde hair flowing around her shoulders. Her blue eyes focused on Mac and then Cole.

"Thanks so much for coming on such short notice. I'm Sedona Reeves. Let me introduce you to everyone." She pointed toward a table where two men had angled their chairs and were playing a game of cards. "The man on the left is Nick Buckley. He's our drummer and also drives the van."

Nick, whose red baseball cap nearly hid his dark eyes, looked up and gave a polite nod. The man was in his early thirties and had dark hair just long enough to curl at the neck below the cap.

"And this is our bass player, Joel Osinski."

"Who likes to cheat at cards," Nick added with a growl.

Joel laughed, a sound somewhere between a chuckle and a cackle, and raised a hand in greeting.

Miss Reeves shook her head, a ghost of a smile on her face. "Then we have Chloe Morse. She plays the keyboard. And finally, this is Lou Gierhart. He handles the soundboard, is our tour manager, and keeps track of a million other things."

Chloe, a short woman in her late twenties who was barely five feet tall, smiled warmly. Lou also stood to shake their hands. The man was in his forties with a thin and wiry frame. He lifted a paper cup of coffee that he held in his left hand. "Can I get you boys some coffee? It's not too bad here."

Cole shook his head. "I'm good, thank you."

Mac turned down the offer as well. He went through everyone's names again in his mind, hoping to remember them all. Not for the first time, he was thankful to have inherited his dad's way with names and faces. It came in handy all the time.

"It's good to meet you all." Mac nodded at them and

turned his focus on the woman standing in front of him. "What's going on, Miss Reeves? I understand you're having trouble with a possible stalker?"

"Please, just call me Sedona. And yes, or at least it seems that way. Would you like to have a seat?" She motioned to a pair of unoccupied chairs. Once Mac and Cole got comfortable, she sat on a chair across from them next to Chloe. "Our first two weeks of the tour were in Arkansas, and we didn't have any trouble there."

Mac noticed that Chloe opened her mouth like she was going to say something, then closed it again. She caught him watching her and quickly focused on her friend instead. He filed that fact away.

Sedona continued. "It wasn't until we entered Oklahoma that weird things started to happen. I've had a few notes left for me to find. Then there are the creepy texts…"

As if suddenly cold, she wrapped her arms around herself and leaned forward. Her hair draped over her shoulders, the ends brushing against her knees. Mac studied her without lingering too long on any one feature. She was clearly an accomplished artist. She walked away from a label to pursue music on her own, showing determination and grit, and she was undeniably beautiful. Any of those three alone might catch the attention of a would-be stalker.

Lou reached for a manila envelope on the side table next to him and handed it to Mac. "I kept the notes. Just in case." He tossed Sedona an apologetic smile.

Interesting. Apparently, by the way she frowned at him, she either had no idea or hadn't thought it was necessary to keep them in the first place.

Mac accepted the envelope and carefully emptied the contents on the small coffee table in front of him and Cole.

All the notes were printed on 4x6 pieces of glossy photo paper. Definitely not a typical way to print anything with text.

There were five of them with no indication of what order they were printed in. He read each one in turn:

"You aren't alone."

"I see you."

"There's always tomorrow."

"Do you dream about me?"

"I need you."

They were all creepy, no doubt about it. Aside from the first, they weren't sinister, and even then, you could put several different spins on the words "You aren't alone."

Cole held the envelope open so Mac could slide them back inside. "Where were these left?"

"The first two were taped to the door of the van." Sedona's eyes focused on the manila envelope. "Two places that hosted concerts had an area for us to prepare. We found them there, too. Then someone slipped a note under the door of my hotel room three days ago." Her blue eyes lifted to Mac's face. "I've gotten a few weird texts, too. Always from an unknown number."

She stood, got her phone out, and swiped at the screen. A moment later, she handed it to him, the text window open.

Unlike the notes that weren't overly personal, the texts were much more so. There had to be at least ten of them.

"May I?"

"Please." Sedona went to sit down again, her hands clasped in her lap.

He and Cole looked through the texts. Several simply asked if she'd gotten his note. But two, especially, stood out.

> You looked beautiful tonight. I loved the red dress.

> What perfume do you wear? It smells amazing.

He couldn't blame her if the notes made her uncomfortable, but these texts were crossing a line. Mac was inclined to take the case just based on them alone. Maybe Asher, their tech whiz brother, could figure out who was sending them. "Have there been any security cameras at any of the locations you could check? See if someone was caught leaving the notes?" He directed the question to Connor.

"Unfortunately, no. The locations where the notes were left had no security cameras within sight of the van. The hotel where the note was passed under the door checked their tapes. The video was of terrible quality. It looked like it might've been a man in a dark jacket with the hood up. And even that was more of an educated guess."

Mac exchanged a look with Cole. "That likely means he's paying attention to his surroundings. Choosing when to act based on that. The fact that he kept his face away from the camera in the hotel likely confirms that."

Cole nodded. "He's doing everything he can to make sure he doesn't get caught. If he's consciously avoiding cameras, he's most likely using a burner phone to send the texts."

Again, Mac spoke directly to Connor. "At what point did you come on board?"

Sedona spoke up. "I made the mistake of mentioning one of the notes to my parents on the phone. They're the ones who insisted on hiring security. No offense, Connor."

"None taken." Connor didn't seem bothered by her comment. "I've been traveling with Sedona and the crew for about ten days now."

"If you've continued to get these notes, then what changed? Why did you call Durham Private Security tonight?"

Everyone else in the room turned to look at Sedona.

She cleared her throat and crossed one knee over the other. "I was hoping he'd stay in Oklahoma. But tonight, after the concert, someone shoved an envelope into my hand. I didn't see him, but this time, the note was different." She visibly shivered. "Chloe suggested getting more security. At first, I thought it might be a bit much. But the more I think about it… Can your company help me?"

THREE

If there was one thing Sedona hated, it was asking for help. Even more so when it came to asking a stranger. What if they thought she was overreacting? What if they were right? Not for the first time, she considered just hanging in there for the rest of the tour. Surely, when she got home, things would return to normal.

Then again, that's what she told herself about when they got back to Texas, too. She hoped and prayed the situation wouldn't deteriorate, yet here they were. The last thing she wanted was to ignore the problem until things went too far, then regret not doing something about it earlier. "I'd like your professional opinion about the situation, no matter what it might be."

The man who introduced himself as Mac studied her for several moments, and there was nothing in his expression to reveal what he was thinking. He ran a hand over his beard and mustache. "What was written in the note?"

She swallowed the lump in her throat and pulled the envelope out of her purse. She handed it over and watched as they read it. She might not have seen the guy when he handed it to her, but he'd clearly been close enough to touch her. That alone was enough to freak her out.

There was a flash of anger on Mac's face. "There's no doubt you have a reason to be concerned. The fact that he went from writing generic notes to sending personal texts is disconcerting. But this note? It's a clear sign of escalation. Especially since he's physically followed you from one state to another, and now he's approaching you in person."

His words lifted a weight from her shoulders that she didn't realize she'd been carrying. He didn't think she was crazy after all. "Does that mean you'll consider the job?"

The two men from Durham Private Security exchanged a silent look that must've conveyed much more than she could decipher because they turned to her at the same time with a nod.

Cole got his phone out and looked at something on the screen. "Is the tour schedule on your website still current?"

"Yes," Lou answered immediately as he leaned forward. "We've been able to stick to the schedule thus far, and I don't see any reason why that shouldn't continue to be the case." He'd been instrumental in setting everything up, from booking their venues to where they were going to stay each night.

"And were you wanting additional security twenty-four hours a day? Or just during performances?" This time, the question came from Mac.

After Chloe had insisted that Sedona consider additional security, she had gone online to look at rates and what was generally included in that. Since they were going to be traveling from town to town, she'd be expected to pay for his room and board along the way. "For the full twenty-four hours, please. We have a section of rooms booked at each hotel we're staying at. We can call ahead and see if we can add another in the same area."

Truthfully, she'd prefer having extra security at night, not to mention in the van while they were traveling. Maybe it wasn't fair, but Connor never did give her an increased sense of safety once he joined the crew.

"We'd like to help you out. If you'll excuse us, we're going to talk it through and put together an estimate for you." Mac got to his feet, closely followed by Cole. Goodness, but they were both tall men, with Mac the tallest by at least three inches. "We'll be back in a few minutes."

"Thank you so much."

The lounge fell silent as the men left the area and then exited the hotel.

"They seem capable," Chloe commented thoughtfully. "And they thought it was a good idea to add security, too." She gave Sedona a pointed look.

Connor's frown deepened. "Of course they did. It means a job and money. I don't think it's necessary to have another person around all the time. Not with me staying here, too. It seems like overkill."

Sedona swallowed back a retort. Connor was only on board because her parents insisted, and she'd rather deal with him than one of them directly.

"I'll be responsible for paying for his hotel rooms whether he's just showing up at concerts or sticking around the whole time. It makes more sense for him to stay close." It was already going to cost her a small fortune. She wasn't willing to risk her safety, or that of those around her, and she wasn't going to allow her parents to add another security detail. If she could afford it, she'd hire two people and dismiss Connor completely. No offense to him personally.

Lou pointed to his phone. "I've been checking out Durham Private Security, and there are plenty of people who highly recommend them. They're definitely legit." Even though he spoke positively about the company, he seemed to be reserved about something.

It was likely the cost. As tour manager, he'd gone over finances with her to make sure their six-week excursion brought in some money. Well, she'd pay for it herself and make sure nothing came out of everyone else's share.

Assuming Mac and Cole came back with something she could remotely afford.

She was on the verge of getting up and looking out the glass hotel doors to make sure they hadn't just driven away when they exited their truck and came back inside. Cole reclaimed his seat.

Mac approached Sedona with a piece of paper in his hand. "Here's a breakdown of our fees. The end charge may be slightly different, but I assure you we always overestimate. This price includes the full support of Durham Private Security. We'd have our technical specialist see if he can figure out who's been sending you the texts. If we have problems with the stalker again, we'll work with local businesses to track down possible video footage or photos. We'll also work with local law enforcement when necessary. If this is agreeable, I personally will be the one accompanying you all."

He still stood in front of her, and his height, along with the impressive width of his shoulders, made her instantly glad he'd be the one protecting her and the band.

For the first time, she really took in his appearance. His brown hair had a slight wave to it and was cut fairly short. It was hard to tell in the dim hotel lighting, but there might be a hint of red, too. What truly struck her, though, was the kindness in his eyes. Yes, he looked serious, and there was a determination that suggested he'd do whatever he had to when it came to keeping her and the rest of the band safe. But underneath all of that was an unmistakable kindness.

First impression? He was every bit the kind of man she'd imagine when she thought of a hero. Second impression? She wouldn't want to meet him in a dark alley, and she'd welcome him on her team any day.

He went to sit down, giving Sedona some time to look over the details and figures on the paper. The cost was higher than she'd guessed but not by much. That said, she'd be getting a lot more than she'd realized, and that included twenty-four-hour help. That wasn't insignificant.

Mac cleared his throat, drawing her attention back to him. "There is one more thing I want to mention. I would insist on accompanying you whenever you leave your hotel room. I will do absolutely everything in my power to keep you safe, and I intend to do exactly that, whether it's here, during a concert, or at the grocery store stocking up on food. I would also prefer to stay in a room that is adjacent to yours."

She could practically feel Connor staring a hole through her but refused to look his way. In the end, this was her decision, and she was going to make it. Besides, after what happened tonight, the thought of Mac shadowing her already gave her a great deal of comfort.

With a decisive nod, she stood and stepped forward. "Agreed." She shook Cole's hand first and then Mac's. While both men's hands were large enough to engulf hers, she hadn't anticipated the combination of safety and awareness that flowed through her when Mac's warm, rough skin touched hers.

She gripped the paper with both hands and shoved the thought away as they went through the many details before signing a contract.

Lou got to his feet. "I'll go speak with the hotel and see if they've got another room for tonight. I'm on one side of Sedona's room, so if there isn't one available, I can swap with you. We haven't been in the rooms long enough to do more than drop off our luggage."

"I appreciate it." Mac jabbed a thumb behind him. "I came prepared and can start immediately. I just need to get my stuff out of the truck."

With that, he and Cole left the hotel again.

Sedona didn't know Mac, but he was clearly capable of taking care of himself. She already felt safer knowing he was traveling with them.

FOUR

"Tomorrow, I'll get everything Asher needs to try and track down the phone the stalker has been texting from." Mac lifted his large duffel bag from the rear seat of his Explorer and slung it over his shoulder. "I'd like to know why they never reported any of this to local police. Or if they did, what was said."

Cole leaned against the side of the Explorer. "Keep an eye on the other security guy, too. Connor doesn't seem thrilled that you're being brought into the middle of things."

"No, he sure doesn't." Mac got the sense that there was a lot about the situation they still didn't know. Chloe had wanted to interject at least once before thinking better about it. He hoped to have the opportunity to ask her a few questions as well. "We'll have Asher do a basic background check on everyone associated with Sedona. The musicians and Connor. Maybe look into the label she was originally with as well."

"Agreed." Cole closed the vehicle door once Mac had gotten everything. "Keep us updated. At least you'll have tomorrow to get a sense of what's going on while you're still in Destiny. We can adjust if necessary before you leave town."

"Sounds like a plan." Mac noticed Cole checking his watch. "You need to get going."

"I promised Peter I would tuck him in tonight. That means he'll be wide awake until I get back, and I know Erica is probably exhausted by now."

Mac smiled as he thought about his nephew. Peter turned nine last month. He and his mom had been on their own until Cole entered the picture last year, when he stepped in to protect them. Cole and Erica got married last summer and seemed happier than ever.

"Then you'd better get going. Maybe stop at the convenience store on the way and pick up a pint or two of ice cream for after he's in bed."

"Now that's a great idea. You got everything you need?"

"Yep." Including his .45 nestled safely in the holster against his lower back. "Take good care of my Explorer."

"Will do." Cole gave Mac a hearty pat on the back. "I'm just a phone call away if you need backup."

Mac waited long enough to watch Cole drive the SUV through the hotel parking lot before making his way back inside.

Sedona gave him a warm smile, but there was a hint of uncertainty in her blue eyes. "Thank you so much. I know this was super short notice. I appreciate you and your team for taking this on."

"Of course. I'll probably have a lot of questions tomorrow." He looked at his watch. It was nearly ten-thirty. "I imagine you're all about ready to call it quits for tonight."

She nodded. "Most of the time, we've all gone to our rooms by now or would soon. Some of us meet in the lobby for breakfast in the morning. Others will sleep in or hit the gym. Either way, we'll meet up here at eleven to go over the day's schedule and make lunch. We've got a large cooler in the van with sandwich fixings. It helps to save money."

Mac noticed that both men who had been playing cards

were already gone. Connor sat nearby and seemed to be engrossed with something on his phone.

Lou and Chloe walked up to join them.

"The best we could get was five doors down from Sedona," Chloe told them.

Lou nodded. "My room is next to Sedona's." He motioned to Mac. "Like I mentioned before, I'm happy to trade with you."

"I appreciate that. What floor are we on?" Mac followed the trio out of the lounge area, past the front desk, and down the hall to the right. Connor trailed behind them.

"Here on the first." Sedona opened her clutch and took out a hotel key card.

Mac would've preferred one of the upper floors simply because it limited access to the rooms. They paused at a door so Lou could open it.

"I'll just grab my stuff quickly, and it'll be all yours." Lou handed over his key card.

He gathered his things while Chloe wished them good night. Lou carried his suitcase past them and further down the hall, leaving the door wide open for Mac to enter.

Connor finally slipped his phone into his pocket and focused on Sedona. "You good?"

She nodded. "Yep. Thanks so much."

With a mumbled "Good night," he walked further down the hall.

Mac entered his new hotel room. He set his duffel bag on the bed and turned the heater down several degrees.

Sedona was standing just inside the room by the door. He went back to join her.

"What's your usual routine in the morning?"

She shrugged. "I go down for breakfast at seven. If you arrive much later than that, all the best stuff is usually picked over. After that, I come back to my room and do anything I need to for the day, then chill until eleven."

"I'd like to accompany you down for breakfast. You sure it won't be too early if I knock on your door at seven?"

"Breakfast is my favorite meal of the day. Trust me, I'll be ready to go."

"Sounds good. I'd appreciate it if you didn't leave your room until then." Mac sounded bossy, and he knew it, but he couldn't protect her if he didn't know where she was. What he didn't want was for her to go down to the pool or the gym without him knowing and not have security there if something were to happen.

Thankfully, she didn't seem offended. If anything, she seemed relieved. "That won't be a problem."

"Good." Mac gave her a nod of approval. "There's something else I need from you." He took his phone out. "I need your number so I can put it in my contacts list and make sure you have mine. If anything happens that concerns you, I want you to call or text me. It doesn't matter what time of the day or night it is."

Her pretty blue eyes widened a little. She told him her number, which he stored on his phone. Then he sent her a text to make sure she got his.

She added his information to her contacts as well. "Okay, I'm all set."

"The last thing I want to do is show you a trick to keep someone from slipping anything under your door. Do you mind if we go in your room real quick?"

"Not at all." She led the way.

He went ahead and closed the door behind them. "We're going to have a wedge for you starting tomorrow. For tonight, you can use the rod out of the closet." He retrieved it for her and then proceeded to the bathroom. "Now, wrap it in a towel." Once he'd finished that, he placed it on the floor next to the bottom of the door. "That'll block the space. Once you've done that, then you can shift a chair up against the rod or even set your suitcase in front. Someone who is going to slip a note under there is going to be moving fast, so they can get out of the hallway before someone sees him. He's not going to take the time to see if he can push this out of the way."

"That's great, thank you."

"You're welcome." Mac glanced around the room. "I'd like to take a quick look at your windows, too. Make sure they're locked."

She nodded and stepped back, leaving behind the faint scent of honeysuckle. He knew the scent well because his parents grew it along a trellis in the backyard. It'd always been one of his favorites.

He shoved the thought away as he passed by and checked the window locks. All were firmly in place.

"Everything looks good."

Hopefully, the others in the band had taken the time to make sure their windows were secure as well. It was going to be interesting keeping track of everyone. If he were Connor, he'd welcome a second person coming in as security because keeping an eye on everything would be a lot otherwise.

Mac reminded himself that his priority was Sedona's safety. As long as he knew where she was and that she was safe, everything else would sort itself out. Especially with the extended help of his family and team.

Sedona covered a yawn with a slender hand. When it finally ended, she chuckled softly. "Sorry about that. It's been an emotionally-charged day. The concert was an amazing experience, but then to deal with whoever keeps following me... It's been a lot."

"I can only imagine." He jabbed a thumb at the door. "I'll get out of your hair. Maybe some rest tonight will help."

"Thank you again. I'm glad you're 0n board."

"Me, too. Good night."

She smiled. "Good night."

Once Mac was in the hallway again, he waited long

enough to hear the deadbolt slide into place and was happy when the light beneath the door was snuffed out with the makeshift door wedge.

In his room, he got out his iPad and made a detailed list of the things he wanted to have on hand before they left town in less than 48 hours. He'd send the list to Cole, who would make sure they had everything.

At the top of the list was a real wedge to put at the bottom of hotel doors, along with two portable security cameras.

After taking a quick shower so he'd be ready for tomorrow, Mac said a prayer for Sedona's safety and rest. Minutes after his head hit the pillow, he was fast asleep.

Two hours later, the muffled sound of a woman's scream jolted him awake.

FIVE

Sedona didn't realize she was screaming until she'd jumped away from the window. Her heel caught on the leg of the chair in front of the tiny desk, and she fell. The moment her back hit the bed frame, the breath whooshed from her lungs.

Someone pounded on her hotel door. "Sedona? Are you okay?"

It took a moment to realize the concerned voice belonged to Mac.

She tried to take in a much-needed breath, but her lungs wouldn't work. Finally, precious oxygen flooded in, and she gasped as she pulled herself to her feet.

"Sedona!"

She grabbed an oversized sweatshirt from the foot of the bed and yanked it on over her head. With a groan of pain, she bent down to move everything away from the base of the door, then opened it to find not only Mac standing there but Connor and Chloe as well.

"There was someone outside my window." Her words sounded breathy, and she inhaled slowly. "It scared me, and I tripped and fell when I backed away from the window." She tried to keep her voice low so she wouldn't wake up any more people in the hotel than she obviously already had.

To his credit, Mac didn't even look surprised. Instead, he jumped into action. "Could you tell what he looked like? Or what he was wearing?"

She shook her head. "He was dressed in all black with a matching ski mask."

He pointed to the door she kept open with one of her feet. "Go back in your room and close the door. Connor—"

"Yep, I've got it."

With a single nod, Mac turned and strode down the hall toward the lobby.

Chloe put an arm around Sedona's shoulders and led her back inside. The door closed behind them, where she assumed Connor was standing guard.

"What happened?" Chloe steered her toward one of the two chairs situated around the tiny table on one side of the hotel room.

Sedona sat down and winced when her sore back rested against the chair. "I was asleep, and something woke me up. I wasn't sure what it was, but then I heard something tapping against the window. I was so tired, I guess I thought maybe it was storming outside. Like it was little pieces of hail. I pulled the blinds back, and there was a man standing there staring at me." She shivered. In hindsight, thunderstorms with hail were rare in December, but her half-asleep brain hadn't registered that fact.

"Did you recognize him?"

"No. But like I told Mac, he was wearing dark clothes and a black ski mask. The lighting wasn't good enough to see much of anything else."

Chloe frowned, her eyes echoing with the concern and fear that Sedona knew were present in her own. "I don't like this. At all. Seriously, this creep is getting bolder."

"I know. I don't like it, either." Sedona was so thankful

Chloe had insisted on calling in someone else to help with security. "Mac said he's going to put more safeguards in place tomorrow. There wasn't a lot he could do tonight on such short notice."

"True." Chloe ran her fingers through her tangled brown hair. "He sure reacted fast, though. There's a lot to be said for that. The fact that he's not hard to look at certainly doesn't hurt, either."

"Chloe!" Sedona's cheeks flamed because her friend was right, even though she wasn't about to admit it out loud.

There was a knock at the door, and Chloe motioned for Sedona to wait. Chloe paused until Mac's voice said something on the other side letting her know it was safe to open. Both Mac and Connor walked in.

Connor shut the door again behind them. "See anyone?"

"Nope." Mac paced to the window and looked out, as though he wanted to get a sense of what she might've seen from inside the room. He strode over to the table and claimed the chair Chloe had just vacated. "Tell me what you saw."

She told him about hearing the tapping noises and seeing a man staring at her through the window. "He was wearing a ski mask. I couldn't tell anything about him. Except he stared right at me." Another shiver went through her.

"Did he say anything? Do anything once you saw him?"

Sedona shook her head. "Nothing. Just stared for a few moments. It startled me, and I stepped back, and my heel caught on the stupid chair." She pointed to the offending piece of furniture. "Did you see anything at all outside to suggest someone was standing out there?"

"He was long gone by the time I left the hotel and got around to that side. He must've been standing in the narrow flower bed, but the area was already trampled on. I'm going to mention it to the manager on shift here so they're aware, but since the guy didn't do anything outside of tapping on your window, there's not much for the police to respond to."

Sedona nodded absently. It made sense. It really was a catch-22. She hoped the stalker never did something bad enough to warrant calling the cops. At the same time, the thought that he was running around out there potentially planning his next move was a scary one.

Connor leaned against a wall with his arms crossed. "No security cameras on that side?"

"I didn't see any. I'll be asking the manager about that as well." Mac ran his hand over his chin. "I'll work with Lou tomorrow to make sure we have future hotel stays reserved on the second or third floors if possible. At least we won't have to worry about anyone lurking outside your room."

"Thank you." Sedona cringed as she looked around the room. "I'm so sorry I woke you all up. Please, get some rest. I'll do my best not to scream bloody murder again tonight."

Her comment earned her a chuckle from Chloe, who gave her a hug of support before leaving to go back to her room. Connor, too, said he was glad Sedona was okay. Once he was gone, it was only Mac and Sedona left in the room.

He watched her closely. Was he expecting her to break down?

The very idea that she'd screamed loud enough to wake Mac and Connor flooded her with embarrassment. She so didn't want to be that woman who freaked out over every little thing. But seriously, when she saw that guy staring at her through the window, it had been instinct. Next time, she'd grab her phone and try to take a picture before he ran away.

Next time.

Boy, she hoped there wouldn't be a next time.

"You said you fell. Are you okay?"

Without even thinking about it, she pressed a hand against the sore spot on her back, right below her ribs on the right side. "I'll be fine. It just knocked the wind out of me for a minute or so."

The concern on his face sharpened. "You should check to

see if there's any bruising. A fall hard enough to knock the wind out of you can cause significant damage if you hit just wrong. May I have a look?"

Her surprise must've shown on her face because he clarified himself.

"If you were injured, we want to make sure you have the chance to see a doctor tomorrow before your performance. I, at least, know where you could get seen before we leave town."

He wasn't wrong.

Sedona stood and swallowed the groan as her side protested. She rotated so the back of her right side was facing Mac and lifted her sweatshirt and pajama shirt just high enough to expose the area that struck the bed frame.

Mac pulled a small flashlight from one of his pockets and clicked it on. She could feel the heat from the beam on her skin as he leaned in for a closer look.

"It's definitely going to bruise."

She nearly jumped when he lightly touched her skin. His fingers were warm and just a little rough as they examined the area. She sucked in a breath.

"Did that hurt?"

"It's sore but not too bad." Sedona wasn't about to admit the inhale was in response to his touch and not because of pain. In fact, she wasn't willing to analyze that herself, either.

Chloe's comments about Mac being nice to look at flashed in her mind, and Sedona's cheeks warmed.

"No swelling, so that's a good sign." He tugged her shirts back down. "If you start experiencing more pain, or you find it hurts to breathe, please say something immediately. I can get you some acetaminophen...

"I've got some in my suitcase. Thank you, though."

Now that they were standing next to each other, he seemed almost bigger than life. She was five foot eight, and he made her feel tiny. Not just because of the difference in height, but the width of his shoulders, too. She wasn't a petite woman, but next to him, she sure felt that way.

He nodded in satisfaction. "Do you think you'll be able to get some sleep?"

Sedona turned her head to look at the window. It was concealed by vertical blinds and thick blackout curtains. Right now, they even looked creepy. "Not yet. But please, don't let that stop you from going back to bed."

He shrugged. "I'll stay and keep you company. Unless you'd rather be alone."

There was nothing in his expression to tell her which he might prefer.

Did she want to be alone? No. What if the guy came back? What if he was waiting for her to fall back to sleep and everything to quiet down just so he could tap on her window again?

SIX

Mac watched as Sedona seemed to weigh her options. He was about to suggest they could go down to the lounge area if she'd rather not be in the room with him when her shoulders rose with a shake of her head.

"No, I don't particularly want to be alone." She motioned to the small table and reclaimed the chair she'd been sitting in before.

"I wouldn't, either, if roles were reversed." He gave her a kind smile as he took the other chair. "I hate asking you this, but it's better if I do while everything is still fresh. Did you notice anything unusual about the guy? The way he moved?"

She thought a moment as she nibbled on her bottom lip. "Unfortunately, there was nothing that stood out. I wish there had been. The lighting wasn't great, and I had just woken up." She gingerly leaned into the back of the seat. "What are the odds this was some random person who thought it'd be funny to pull off a stupid prank?"

"Since he was wearing a ski mask, I'd say it's highly unlikely." Besides, if someone from the concert had wanted to track her down, he probably would've wanted her to see his face: make it so the famous singer recognized him. This was more than someone being mischievous or acting on a spur-of-the-moment dare.

She rubbed her eyes with her hands and stifled a yawn. "I suppose running after peeping Toms in the dark is an everyday occurrence for you."

He chuckled. "Not exactly, but I'll admit this wasn't the first time."

Sedona looked exhausted, but she didn't seem to be in a hurry for him to leave. "So, since your last name is Durham, does that mean you run Durham Private Security?"

"It's a family business, actually. There are quite a few Durhams involved." He flashed her a smile. "My parents own it, and my brothers and sister work there in different capacities."

"And Cole?" She must've remembered he had a different last name.

"He's my half-brother."

"Which of you is older?"

Mac pointed to his chest. "By two years."

"That's neat that you all get along well enough to work together like that." Her voice sounded wistful.

"I take it that's not true of your family."

"No." That one word was punctuated by a humorless chuckle. "I grew up hearing about how having a child was so much work. Then, when I wanted to pursue a career in music, how childish I was being. That it was a complete waste of my time and the money they poured into my education."

"I'm sorry to hear that. No kid should be made to feel like a burden."

"No, they shouldn't."

Silence descended on the room. Sedona seemed to be wrestling with her thoughts, and Mac gave her the time she needed.

Finally, she dragged her focus from the table between

them to his face. "I have a strange request regarding Connor. He seems capable enough, but he was hired by my parents. I basically accepted the help to keep them from coming down here and getting in the middle of everything themselves. I think he reports everything that happens back to them." She picked at a spot on the table where the varnish had been scratched off. "I'm not saying you should go behind his back, but if it's possible to share information while he's not in the room, I'd appreciate it."

"Of course."

Interesting.

He hadn't been sure what to think of Connor before, other than getting the sense that the man didn't quite put the importance on his job that Mac thought he should. Was it possible that he was sent by her parents under the pretense of security and that Sedona's safety wasn't his first priority? Mac made a mental note to check into their backgrounds as well.

"Thank you." She yawned again, and this time, there was no trying to stop it. Her eyes were watering by the time she'd finished. "I'm sorry. As much as I don't want to, I think I'm going to have to get some sleep."

"It's the adrenaline fading." He knew that feeling of exhaustion after a stressful event well. He pushed away from the table and stood. "I'll go and let you get some rest."

Sedona stood as well and walked him to the door.

Mac opened it and paused. "If you need anything, feel free to call, text, or knock on my door. If you think someone is messing with your window again, let me know. I'll go around outside and try to catch him in the act." He almost hoped the guy tried it again.

"I appreciate it. I hope you're able to get some sleep, too. See you at seven?"

"I'll be here."

When the door closed behind him, he waited long enough

to hear the lock slide in place and see that she put the makeshift wedge at the bottom of the door again before going back into his room. He sent another e-mail to Asher asking him to look into Sedona's parents, in addition to the rest of the band members and Connor, and then settled in for a few hours of sleep before his alarm would go off at six-thirty.

When Mac knocked on Sedona's door promptly at seven in the morning, he'd expected her to appear looking tired and maybe a bit bedraggled. At least that's how Livi handled a combination of late nights and early mornings.

Instead, the door opened, and Sedona stepped out looking as though she'd had all the time in the world to get ready. She wore a pair of dark blue jeans and a pale blue sweater that reminded him of a frozen lake. It made her blue eyes pop even more. Her hair hung down her back in waves.

"I hope you were able to get some sleep after I left."

She nodded. "It took me a few minutes, but I slept solid until my alarm went off."

Mac refrained from asking what time her alarm had been set for. "I'm glad to hear it."

He'd slept okay as well, although maybe not as soundly as he might have normally. Still, he'd gotten more than enough rest to function for the day.

Together, they made their way down the hallway toward the dining area, where a large breakfast had been set out for guests. Joel, Lou, and Nick were already eating at a table in the far corner. They waved their greetings.

Sedona went through the buffet-style breakfast, and Mac followed. She walked away with a pancake drowned in syrup, some scrambled eggs, a sausage patty, and a large helping of fresh fruit.

Mac's plate looked similar, except he got two pancakes and double the scrambled eggs.

There wasn't enough room to sit with Joel and the others, so Sedona snagged another table that had just become available. Mac took the seat across from her, and they dug into their breakfasts.

Conversation was limited. Between eating and the ambient noise as other guests trickled in for breakfast, it would've been hard to hear much.

Chloe walked in, got a bagel and some fruit, and joined them. Connor was the last to arrive. He shot them a look that was impossible to interpret and went straight for the coffee.

Mac waited until the other security guard was well out of earshot. "Does he normally arrive at things like this later than you?" He directed the question to Sedona.

"Occasionally. Most of the time, though, he's waiting for me when I leave my room. He probably figured he didn't need to now that you're here." She glanced at Connor and frowned. "Though we never had an official conversation about it."

Mac wondered whether Connor felt like Mac was stepping on his toes, or if he was glad to have him take over the primary job of keeping Sedona safe.

Connor approached their table with a cup of coffee in one hand and a packaged pastry in the other. He grunted as he sat in the last available chair.

The pancakes were quite good. Mac wished he'd grabbed a third one, but this would be plenty. "So, what are the plans for today? What time do you need to be at the venue for tonight's concert?"

He'd checked the schedule again this morning, and they were supposed to perform at Destiny Christian University at six in the evening.

"We need to be there at four so Lou has plenty of time to get everything set up with sound and all." Chloe smeared some cream cheese on her bagel. "Until then, it just depends. Some people may hang out at the hotel and get laundry done or relax. Sometimes, some of us will go shopping for snacks or anything else we might need."

Sedona nodded. "One afternoon, we all went to see a movie at this cool old theater. When we get to Houston, I want to try to make it to the beach. We scheduled the tour so we'd have the rest of the day once we get to a location to just relax and do some sightseeing or whatever." Her eyes lit up, and she seemed to forget all about the rest of her meal. "I haven't been to the coast since I was a kid. So, if there's one thing we make time for while we're there, that has to be it."

Mac imagined that, with only one vehicle, often the majority ruled when it came to deciding what to do and where to go when they weren't performing. Well, he'd go wherever Sedona went.

He ate the last of his breakfast and washed it down with the rest of his orange juice. "I'll be hearing from Cole later this morning. Our tech expert, Asher, is looking into several things, and we should have an update before we leave town tomorrow morning."

There was no missing the curiosity on Connor's face.

Mac hoped they might be able to keep the meeting small and include only himself, Cole, Asher, and Sedona. Even though all her bandmates seemed nice enough, as far as Mac was concerned, everyone was a suspect until proven otherwise.

SEVEN

Joel lowered his voice so only Sedona could hear it. "I'm not trying to tell you what to do. I'm just saying that, as much as I agree that extra security is necessary, footing the bill yourself is going to really cut into what you're bringing home after all of this."

"That might be true, but I don't want to do nothing and wish later that I'd made a different choice." Which meant she'd be paying for security out of her own profits. As the lead singer, it was more than everyone else was getting. Still, though, it was going to be painful. She'd get through the rest of the tour and pay Durham Private Security, then she'd deal with what happened next when it happened. "None of what's happening is your fault. Or Chloe's or Nick's or Lou's. You guys shouldn't have to take a pay cut for it."

"It's not your fault, either." Joel's voice was firm. "I'm just saying it might be worth letting your parents cover the cost of additional security."

"That's not going to happen. Right now, we need to focus on finishing the tour. Everything will sort itself out later."

He didn't look convinced, but his gaze shot over to the

door of the hotel's laundromat where Mac had entered the room.

He'd gotten a phone call a few moments earlier and had excused himself to the hallway. Sedona wasn't sure if it was because of the noise of the laundromat or because he'd wanted to speak to whoever was on the phone in private. Most likely, it was a little of both.

Mac looked from Joel to Sedona but said nothing. He didn't miss much. "That was just Cole checking in. How's your back feeling this morning?"

She placed her palm against the bruise that she'd examined in the mirror as soon as she woke up. While it was an ugly shade of purple, the dimensions of it hadn't gotten any bigger. "Sore, but I'll be fine. Thanks for asking."

He motioned to her neatly folded pile of laundry. "Are you waiting on another load?"

"No, this is it." She hated to leave Joel alone.

As if he could read her mind, he waved her on. "I'm only going to be another fifteen minutes."

"Okay. If you're sure."

When Joel nodded, Sedona placed her laundry into a large bag to make it easier to carry. Immediately, Mac reached for the bag and shouldered it. His bicep bulged, the muscle straining against the sleeve of his shirt.

"Thank you."

The guy was handsome, determined, clearly in control of the situation, and he was a gentleman. Attraction flared, and she pushed it away immediately. He was here because he had a job to do, and once the tour was over, she'd likely never see him again. She needed to remember that.

Mac opened the door that led to the hallway, looked out, then let her pass by him. "It's not a problem." He led the way toward their hotel rooms. "I'm having Asher—he's the IT tech we mentioned—do a background check on a few people connected to your tour. We should have some information and updates for you this afternoon."

They made it to her room, and he waited patiently while she unlocked the door. He followed her inside and set the bag of clean laundry on the small table.

"If you agree, I'd like for Cole to swing by at two to pick us up and take us to Durham Private Security headquarters to go over the findings."

She hadn't been expecting that. "We'll have to be at the university two hours later. Will there be time to do that and get back to the hotel?"

"We're only fifteen minutes away, and we'll make the meeting relatively fast. You'd mentioned not wanting Connor to hear everything. Plus, and I'm going to be upfront with you, I'm having background checks run on everyone associated with the tour. It might be less awkward if they weren't around for the conversation."

He watched her as though he wasn't sure how she was going to react.

At first, Sedona wanted to object. Or at least ask that Chloe and Joel join them. But if she did that, then the others would wonder why they were being excluded.

Mac was probably right. If they had to have a conversation about each member of the team, then it would be better to do it somewhere else.

Finally, she nodded. "Yeah. That sounds fine."

He smiled and looked relieved. "Great, I'll let Cole know. It'll be good, too, because you'll get the chance to meet some of the others. Then they'll be familiar for future video conferences."

Wow, they really were professional. She was super curious to meet some of Mac's family members.

Sedona's jaw dropped as their vehicle drove down a long driveway and approached a ginormous two-story home. She stared out the window from the backseat and took in all the details. She heard Cole refer to it as "The Castle" earlier, and she figured it might be some kind of private joke. Now she could see that it was exactly what it looked like.

"Do you guys live here? Or is it just the base of operations?"

"Most of us do. Not this guy, though." Mac reached across the console and shoved Cole good-naturedly. "He up and moved away after he got married last year."

Cole looked at her in the rearview mirror. "I live nearby with my wife, Erica, and our son, Peter." He smiled, and it was clear he was more than happy about that fact. "Everyone else lives here for now. Though it's rare to catch them all at home at the same time. Someone's usually traveling on assignment."

Like Mac was now. It made more sense to have someone live there and take care of the property.

"Still, it seems huge. Did you have it built?"

Mac twisted slightly in his seat so he could see her better. "No, but we did have it renovated. It used to be a boys' home. We have permanent living quarters for those of us who stay here, but we also have some furnished guest rooms in case one of our clients needs a safe place to lie low until their situation has been sorted out."

Like a well-protected bed and breakfast. Impressive.

Cole pulled up to the large, covered porch. "Our sister, Livi, is excited to meet you in person. You spoke to her when you called originally. She's been a fan of yours for years."

For whatever reason, the thought that Livi liked her music made Sedona feel even more nervous about meeting the Durham clan. Sedona wondered whether Mac had heard any of her music, not that it really mattered. Or at least, it shouldn't.

As impressive as the outside of the house was, the inside was even more so. They entered a foyer that opened into a great room with a gorgeous fireplace in the corner. Near one wall was a full Christmas tree that stood at least seven feet high. It was filled with white and blue lights and ornaments that gave the entire room a homey feel.

She took in the garland over the doorways and the way the room smelled of fresh pine and cinnamon.

"Wow, this is gorgeous." Sedona didn't intend to sound quite so wistful. To think they all celebrated Christmas together. Or at least she assumed they did. She remembered the last Christmas she spent with her parents, but it wasn't a happy memory. She shoved the comparison aside.

"I'm not sure which of our parents loves Christmas decorations more." Mac chuckled. "Speaking of…"

Sedona's attention was drawn to a couple as they entered the great room. Both wore warm smiles as they approached.

The man, who was nearly as tall as his sons, looked very much like an older version of Mac. He held out his hand to shake hers. "I'm Greg Durham, and this is my wife, Ruth."

To Sedona's surprise, Ruth stepped forward and gave her a hug.

"It's wonderful to meet you, Sedona. I'm glad you were able to come in before you continue your tour. Had you been to Destiny before?"

Sedona immediately relaxed. "It's wonderful to meet you both. No, this is the first time. I really like it, though. It's large enough to have everything you need, but it doesn't feel like a big city. Have you guys lived here long?"

"Only a little over a year, but we like it a lot." Ruth motioned for Sedona to follow her. "Can I get you something to drink? We've got hot tea, coffee, and hot chocolate."

"Tea would be wonderful, thank you."

Ruth's eyes lit up. "Of course. If you'll come with me, I'll show you what kinds we have."

A handful of minutes later, Sedona was escorted into a large dining room with a cup of cinnamon apple herbal tea in her hands.

The center of the room was filled with one of the largest tables she'd ever seen. It looked like it was made of oak, and there were matching chairs lined up along both sides, as well as one at each end.

Sitting around the table were two men and two women. All of them looked up expectantly, their expressions friendly and welcoming.

Mac motioned to a man who was sitting behind a laptop that he'd pushed aside when she entered the room. "This is Asher. He's our IT guru and the one who's been helping with your case since yesterday evening."

Asher gave her a wave. "Hey, it's good to meet you." He pushed his dark-rimmed glasses higher on the bridge of his nose.

"You, too." She smiled and turned her attention to the woman sitting a couple of chairs down.

"And that's Livi, our sister. She does a little of everything and keeps things running smoothly."

The pretty woman's cheeks reddened as she gave a shy smile. "Welcome. I'm the one who spoke to you on the phone when you called. I'm glad our company fits your needs." Her hair was a chestnut brown that fell to the middle of her back. She, Asher, and the other man at the table shared similar features, and both clearly took after their mother.

"I am, too. Thank you for setting everything up."

"Of course."

Mac motioned toward the other man and woman she hadn't met yet. "This is Gavin, another brother." They all chuckled. "He just wrapped up a case less than a month ago, which is how he met Ivy Ramsey."

Gavin reached over and took Ivy's hand. Clearly, there

was a story there. "It's great to meet you, Sedona. You're in good hands." He absently scratched his trimmed goatee.

Ivy nodded enthusiastically, her light brown, wavy hair bouncing gently. "I wouldn't be here if it weren't for them. I can't recommend them enough." She looked at Gavin then with an expression that left no doubt she cared a great deal about him.

"You guys heading out?" The question came from Greg.

Gavin stood and, still holding Ivy's hand, helped her to her feet. He addressed Sedona. "We really wanted to meet you, and I'm sorry we're leaving so quickly."

Ivy stopped to retrieve a purse from the floor. "My brother, Truitt, is flying in today after being deployed for the last nine months. We're driving to Killeen to meet him at the airport and bring him back." There was no missing her excitement. "It really was wonderful to meet you, Sedona."

"You, too. Enjoy the visit with your brother."

With that, Gavin and Ivy left the dining room.

Mac pulled a chair out for Sedona to sit, then he and Cole took chairs on either side of her.

Ruth placed a plate of Christmas cookies on the table in front of Sedona and went to sit next to Greg.

Asher cleared his throat. "I know you're on a tight schedule, so I figured we'd jump right into it." He absently tapped a finger against the laptop. "I've been going through records for your parents, Connor, and your bandmates. I thought we'd start with—"

"Wait, what?" Sedona blinked at him, unsure she'd heard him right, and turned to look at Mac. She set her teacup down on the table with a clink. "Why are you looking into my parents?" She'd never asked them to do that. What did they have to do with anything?

Mac put a calming hand on her arm. "Sedona, we have no real leads. It's important we look into everyone connected with you and your band, and that includes your parents."

EIGHT

The confusion on Sedona's face morphed into disbelief and then suspicion. It was that last expression that bothered Mac the most. He could kick himself for not warning her that they were going to be looking into her parents and not just Connor.

"We aren't saying they're responsible or even connected to what's been going on during your tour." He hoped his calm voice would reassure her. "But I am concerned about Connor, and we needed to know how he was hired, who he works for, and how your parents found out about that company in the first place."

The muscles in her arm tightened beneath his palm as she gripped the edge of the table.

Livi leaned forward. "I'm sorry. I know this can all be disconcerting. Nothing like having virtual strangers dig into the people in your life. I'm sure you get enough of that with social media and all."

Sedona's arm shifted away from Mac as she ran both of her hands through her hair. She gathered it at the base of her neck and pulled it over one shoulder before releasing it again. "No, it's okay. I just didn't realize... Please, go ahead."

Her tea apparently forgotten, she fiddled with a silver ring around her left pointer finger, the motion revealing her uncertainty.

Asher exchanged a look with Mac, who nodded for him to continue.

"Connor Pascal works for a private security company in the Houston area. They tend to be hired for positions in malls, jewelry stores, and banks. It doesn't look like a situation like this, traveling personal security, is common for that company. I was unable to find a direct connection between it and Richard and Pamela Reeves."

"That doesn't surprise me. However, my father works in banking with clients both in the United States and overseas. Anyone could've mentioned the company in passing. He may have even hired Connor as a favor for someone. Networking. Most of what he does usually has some tie back into his business."

There was no bitterness in Sedona's voice. Just a quiet acceptance that made Mac upset on her behalf. Had Richard Reeves sacrificed a relationship with his daughter for that same reason?

"What about Connor specifically?" The question came from Cole.

Asher straightened slightly in his chair. "I can't get a look at his bank account or anything like that, but he and his wife did file for Chapter 13 bankruptcy last year. I can only guess as to why, but I can tell you they live in a small apartment, and his wife works in retail."

Mac thought over his interactions with Connor, not that there'd been many yet. "He might have been willing to take a somewhat unconventional job if it paid well enough." Going to protect Sedona and mostly reporting everything back to the Reeves might not be completely ethical, but Connor wasn't doing anything illegal.

"I only agreed to his accompanying us because my parents

insisted and paid for it. If I hadn't, my father threatened to make the trip himself." Sedona frowned. "I didn't think he actually would. I'm not even sure he's in the states right now. But I agreed so they'd quit trying to convince me to cancel the tour and go home."

Cole reached for one of their mom's frosted gingerbread cookies. "Do your parents routinely try to get you to walk away from the music industry?"

Sedona glanced at Mac and hesitated. "They never wanted me to go down this path, but it's all I've ever wanted since I was a little kid. I recorded a few songs and put them up on YouTube in my late teens. The encouragement from listeners kept me going. I recorded more things, found new platforms to get them out into the world, and eventually, one of them went viral. That's what led to labels contacting me to sign with them. It wasn't until then that my parents thought maybe what I was doing was worthwhile." Bitterness clashed with sadness in her tone.

Mac couldn't fathom offering such conditional support for his own child.

"What about when you decided to go independent?" Livi's voice was soft and full of compassion.

"They said it was the biggest mistake of my life." Sedona shrugged as though it wasn't a big deal, but their dismissal of her interests and decisions had clearly done its damage.

It was probably best if Mac never met them, because if they said something negative, he doubted he'd be able to hold his tongue. With what he knew of them, it sounded like it wouldn't be outside the realm of possibility for them to try to scare Sedona into leaving the music industry. "I'm sorry to hear that."

"It is what it is." She chose a tree-shaped gingerbread cookie from the plate and took a bite. Her eyes widened. "Wow, this is amazing."

Mom smiled happily. "Thank you. I make a batch a week through the holidays to keep up with this crew."

Those who hadn't gotten a cookie yet took that opportunity to choose one for themselves. Once they'd settled again, Asher continued.

"Have you had any trouble with Moonlight Studios since you left?"

"I did right at first. When they originally signed me on, I don't think the owner, Gilbert Remming, thought it was going to go anywhere. He only committed to a year and a single album. After that came out, and it seemed to pick up some speed, he extended that to two more. By the end of the last one, he was pressuring me into crossing over from Christian music into the secular market. That's why I decided not to extend our contract beyond that. It was at that point that Gilbert was very upset and told me that I couldn't make it without Moonlight Studios behind me." Sedona took another bite of her cookie and dusted her hands off.

"Well, I listened to you before and after you decided to go independent." Livi leaned forward. "If anything, your music since then is even better."

"Thank you for that." Sedona cleared her throat and seemed to need a moment to compose herself. "It was by the grace of God that I got to where I was before, and I wasn't about to walk away from Him because it was going to sell more albums."

"That's admirable." Their dad's deep voice rumbled from the other side of the table. "Did you ever have trouble with Gilbert Remming threatening you or trying to contact you in a way that wasn't professional?"

"Only right at the beginning. He called twice to tell me I wouldn't be where I was if it weren't for him and his company. After the second time, I asked him not to call me again, and he never did."

If Sedona had gone viral with one of her songs before

Gilbert signed her on, clearly she'd had the talent ahead of time. Mac was willing to bet Gilbert knew that and was aware that she would continue to build her career with or without him.

Asher leaned toward his laptop screen. "I didn't do a deep dive, but my initial look into Moonlight Studios didn't reveal any problems. They don't seem to be having obvious financial difficulties. If they haven't bothered you for nearly two years now, hopefully that means none of this is tied to them."

Sedona gave a nod of satisfaction as she finished her cookie. "I never was in breach of contract, and once it was obvious that I had no intention of going back, I think Gilbert cut all ties."

Mac needed to ask another question, and he prayed she wouldn't find it too intrusive. "Have you had any relationships over the last year or two that didn't end well? A boyfriend who was reluctant to walk away?"

Her cheeks immediately turned a pretty shade of pink, and she ducked her head just slightly. "Wow, you guys definitely check all angles." Her laughter was a little forced.

"I'm sorry, dear," Mom said from the other side of the table. "But in our line of work, we've often found that unrequited love—whether real or imagined—is a big motivator when it comes to cases related to stalking."

"No, it makes sense. I just wasn't expecting that." She drained the rest of her tea and set the cup back down on the table with a bit of a clatter. "There haven't been any relationships for a while. Things have been stressful, and I've spent all my spare time writing or recording in the studio."

Mac got the sense that she might regret that a little. Was there someone she wished she'd made time for?

Sedona swept some of her hair behind her right ear. "Back at the very beginning of my contract with Moonlight Studios, Gilbert kept trying to get me to go to dinner with him or work late after everyone went home. It was clear he had more than work in mind. He was married. I immediately let him know that I wasn't interested, and he acted like he'd never said anything in the first place. No surprise, he and his wife divorced a few years ago."

"How about anyone in the band now?"

Mac's follow-up question made the poor woman blush again.

"Nothing official, but I've wondered if Nick was interested in me. Chloe brought it up a time or two, so I don't think it was just me. He's never said anything. Other than that, there hasn't been anyone."

Mac hadn't noticed Nick paying Sedona any extra attention, but he would be watching for it now.

It was hard for him to believe that someone hadn't pursued a relationship with Sedona. From what he could see, she was kind, firm in her convictions, and beautiful. The kind of beauty that was more than just skin deep. It made a person want to get to know her.

Truthfully, she was totally his type. If he'd met her under other circumstances, he might consider asking her out himself.

The moment that thought entered his head, he shoved it aside. She was a client. Besides, the last woman he'd had in his life had walked away without looking back. Being married and divorced before the age of twenty-five had a way of making him reluctant to ever go down that path again.

Just thinking of falling for someone who traveled regularly for tours and such made his stomach clench.

No, it didn't matter how attracted he was to Sedona Reeves. His job was to protect her until they figured out who was threatening her. Then they'd go their separate ways.

NINE

Sedona may not have known what to expect when she walked into the Durham home, but answering questions about her love life—or lack thereof—had totally thrown her off guard. It made sense they wanted to know about that part of her life, but she definitely wasn't prepared to talk about it with a bunch of strangers.

"I didn't get the rejected suitor vibe from the guy who's been following me. I mean, if he had a crush on me or something, wouldn't he try to approach me and see if I'd be interested first? It seems like writing creepy notes and sending weird texts kinda ensures I'm not going to respond in a positive way."

She'd had several fans who'd approached her over the years. A few lighthearted shouts of "I love you!" from the crowd. She'd never had a man try to get her to notice him or go out with him. Certainly not like that.

It was always fine, too. She was busy focusing on her career. Her dream. The direction she felt like God was leading her in her life. The chance to fall in love, get married, and have a family was way off in the distance.

Yet, through it all, she could never quite shake the negative remarks from her parents about how being flighty was no way to attract a husband.

She must've been silent for too long because everyone was watching her. She covered her embarrassment by reaching for another cookie.

"You're probably right," Mac spoke from the seat to her right. "Most likely he would've tried to get you to notice him by giving you a gift or trying to impress you in some way, which is why this isn't playing out like your typical stalker situation. The hostility has me concerned." He hesitated for a moment. "Sedona, when I first met you and your crew, you mentioned you'd started having issues once you left Arkansas and entered Oklahoma. It looked like Chloe was about to add something and changed her mind. Do you know what that might have been about?"

She broke the cookie in half but then set it down on a napkin near her empty teacup. As if that were a cue, Ruth Durham went to the kitchen and returned with a fresh tea bag and some more hot water. Sedona nodded her thanks.

Yes, she knew exactly what Mac was referring to.

"Chloe is convinced that we started having problems with the stalker in Arkansas. After our second concert, we came out to find that two of the trailer tires were flat. There was a large puncture that could have been caused by anything from a stick to a screwdriver. We never did find what actually caused the damage."

"And Chloe thought someone had destroyed the tires on purpose?"

"She and Joel wondered about that, but there was no evidence either way. It seemed much more possible that we simply ran over something on the way into the parking lot." She'd convinced herself of that, too. Now, looking back, she felt much less certain.

"Was there anything else after that?" Mac's attention never left her face.

"We had a hotel room that was broken into while we were away. But it was one of four in the same hotel, and the rest weren't in our block. Nothing was stolen that we know of. That's it, though."

"What town was this in? Did the hotel report the situation to the local police?" Asher asked.

"Little Rock. Yes, everyone who was renting a room that had been broken into gave a statement."

Mac looked across the table at Asher and gave him a nod. "We'll find out if that report is available."

"You guys agree with Chloe and Joel? That it's all connected?"

"It's certainly suspicious. You've had more than your fair share of bad luck on this trip."

He wasn't wrong, and Sedona was starting to feel silly for not taking the possibility seriously. She finally reached for one half of her cookie and munched on it, thankful for something else to focus on.

Asher typed something on his laptop. "All right, I'll search for that report. I still need to do some research on Nick and Lou. It was almost impossible to find anything on Joel. He doesn't have any social media accounts, which surprised me. That's pretty rare these days, especially for a man in his thirties."

Sedona used a spoon to remove the teabag from the cup and set it on a napkin. "Joel hates everything about the internet. He's convinced computers and AI are going to take over the world." She chuckled. "We've had musicians come and go, but Joel, Chloe, and I have been together since the beginning. Truthfully, being a mountain climber or a farmer in the Australian outback would fit his personality more than playing bass for us."

Everyone around the table laughed.

"Sounds like he and I are on very different ends of the

spectrum," Asher said with a grin. "The only other person I was able to do a search on was Chloe."

"After my song first went viral years ago, I reached out looking for a couple of people who were interested in trying to make a go of breaking into the music industry. I met Chloe first, and then several months later, Joel." Everything had fallen into place at the time. "Chloe was another big reason why I left Moonlight Studios. They wanted to drop her so that I'd be the only woman in the group, and I wasn't willing to do that."

If it hadn't been for Chloe being there and cheering her on, and Joel's stoic support, Sedona wouldn't be where she was. Not to mention, they were both talented musicians.

"Look, I appreciate you all being thorough, but you don't need to worry about Chloe. Seriously."

"I didn't see anything concerning," Asher confirmed. "Like you said, though, we're simply trying to cover all the bases. It's impossible for me to do anything halfway. I'll let you know what I find out about the others."

"It's true." Greg chuckled. "Been that way since he was born."

If the comment bothered Asher, he didn't let on.

There were a few moments of silence before Mac placed his palms on the table. "I think that's it for now. I just wanted to make sure you had a chance to meet everyone before we leave town. I do need to get a few supplies before we head out. It won't take long. I want to make sure you get to the university in plenty of time."

"That sounds good."

"I'll give you a hand," Cole said as the two men stood and left the room.

Sedona looked around the table. "Thank you all for your help. I truly appreciate it."

"Of course." Ruth gave her a warm smile that had Sedona's heart aching.

She barely knew the woman but had the sense that she was probably one of those moms who baked and spent time with her kids and who looked forward to when they got home from school. About the polar opposite of her own.

"Above all," Greg began, "we'll be praying for you."

She gave him a nod of thanks. "It was nice to meet you all."

Asher looked up with a smile. "You, too." Everyone but him stood.

Livi motioned to a large doorway that led from the dining room. "The guys won't take long. If you'd like, we can wait in the living room for them to get back."

Ruth gave Sedona a small hug before she and Greg went in the direction of the kitchen. Sedona followed Livi through the doorway and into the great room where the fireplace was still roaring.

They took a seat on the large couch facing the hearth.

Livi clasped her hands together on her lap. "I just wanted to say how much I respect you for walking away from the label like you did. It couldn't have been easy. Your standing up for what you believe in is a true inspiration."

"I appreciate that." Sedona was deeply touched by the woman's kind comments but also a little thrown. Funny how much easier it was to stand in front of an audience and sing than it was to talk to someone one-on-one and accept a compliment. "A lot has changed in the music industry in the last few years. It's hard to keep up with. I'm thankful I have a great group of people to go through all of it with me."

Livi looked like she was about to say something else when her phone rang. Her face fell momentarily when she read the name on the screen. "I'm so sorry. This is for another case, and I've been waiting for this person to get back to me. You'll be okay in here?"

"Of course. Go. I'll just wait here and admire the Christmas tree until Mac gets back."

The younger woman reached over, gave Sedona's hand a squeeze, and said, "I'll be praying for you, too." She stood and answered the phone on her way out of the room.

After being surrounded by six people in the dining room, the great room seemed suddenly quiet and empty. Sedona got to her feet and wandered to the giant Christmas tree.

As she got closer, she spotted plenty of matching ornaments. For every one of those, however, there was another ornament that had clearly been made by hand.

She imagined Mac and his siblings sitting around a table as they crafted snowmen and candy canes to hang on the tree. Did they have steaming mugs of hot chocolate while Christmas music played in the background?

An intense longing hit her hard, combined with the grief of what she had never experienced, and before she knew it, tears were pooling in her eyes.

Footsteps approached, and she turned her head away slightly so she could subtly swipe at the moisture.

"Hey. Are you okay?" Mac paused just to the right and behind her.

She wasn't subtle enough, apparently.

"Yeah. I guess everything just hit me all at once."

"I can only imagine how stressful this must be for you."

Sedona wanted to shrug her emotions off, but his kind words and steady voice just brought the tears back. With a heavy sigh, she brushed them away.

"It's the tree, actually." She tried to laugh softly, but it came out as more of a half-sob, which she hated. She disliked crying in front of anyone, but especially in front of a man she barely knew. "It's ridiculous, but seeing the tree with all of these fun ornaments and your family all together, it made me suddenly remember the Christmases as a child where I wished I had siblings and trees and all of this." She waved a hand to encompass the room in general.

Mac set something down on the couch before taking

several steps forward. He turned so that he could see her face. "Your family didn't celebrate Christmas?"

"We did. Technically. We had a tree with a one-color theme that I was forbidden to touch. There were no crafts or popping popcorn and watching Christmas movies. No touring Christmas lights or reading stories. When Christmas dinner was over, and presents were opened, they went back to normal, and I returned to entertaining myself and dreaming that things were different. It was…"

"Lonely."

"Yeah. It was lonely." She sniffed, and her shoulders fell a little. "I always vowed that, if I ever had kids, I'd make the entire Christmas season magical for them." Even she was aware of the melancholy tone in her voice. She raised her chin a little to look at Mac.

His hazel eyes, which looked more green today, held a kindness that was almost too much for her. "I have no doubt about that. Look at what you've accomplished so far in your life, and much of it was while facing adversity. I believe you can do anything you set your mind to. Your kids will be blessed to have you for their mom."

"Thank you for that." She drew in a slow breath and let it back out again. "I shouldn't complain. I have my maternal grandmother in my life now. She and my mom were estranged for many, many years. I didn't get to meet her until I was twenty-two. We stay in touch, even if we don't get to see each other often." That was probably way more information than he wanted. She tried to find a way to change the subject and noticed the items on the couch, including a large canvas bag. "What's in there?"

"Some video camera equipment. I'm hoping we can get our hotel rooms swapped to the second or third floors. But if we can't, we're going to have video recordings of anyone else who tries to mess with your window." He pointed to something else. "I also have the wedge to block the bottom of your doors. This will be much easier for you to use."

His words brought Sedona's mind back to the night before, and a cloud of worry descended over her. She focused on the flames as they slowly ate away at the wooden logs in the fireplace. Eventually, they'd be reduced to nothing but ash.

Her thoughts must've shown on her face because Mac reached out and lightly touched her arm. "Sedona? I won't let anything happen to you."

His firm voice snagged her attention and brought it back to him. She had no doubt that he'd do everything possible to keep her safe. The problem was that he wouldn't always be with her.

What if the stalker didn't stop bothering her after the tour was over? What if this was all just the beginning?

What if her idea of a normal life was slowly turning to ash, too?

TEN

Ever since leaving the castle, Sedona seemed unusually quiet. Mac didn't know her well enough to guess whether she was still feeling sad about the holidays, if she was worried about the stalker, or if she was simply focused on the concert later that evening. More than likely, it was some combination of everything.

Once they all loaded up into the van—which was an impressive vehicle in its own right—and were headed to Destiny Christian University, Sedona started to smile again as jokes were tossed back and forth between her and the others.

Nick drove the van, and Connor sat up front with him.

Apparently, Sedona usually sat in the second row. Mac suspected Chloe might have as well, but she moved to the next row back, giving Mac a seat on the same row with only one in between them.

Joel, Lou, and Chloe took up the third row. The seats in the fourth row were laying down so they could store luggage, coolers, and other items in the large space in the back.

"I've seen these Transit vans, but I've never been in one until now. They're huge." Mac counted twelve seats total.

Nick looked at him in the rearview mirror. "Took some

time to get used to driving it, too, especially with the trailer in tow. It's not a big deal now, though. It's a pretty smooth ride."

"I'll say." There was plenty of room between seats with great air conditioning as well. It was a comfortable way to travel. "When my family traveled for vacation, it got crowded. We had a van, but with six kids, that meant someone always had to be crammed in the middle."

Joel, who was in the middle of the third row, chuckled. "And I'll bet the seats weren't nearly as roomy as these are."

"No, they were not. Which is why the youngest always got that spot, whether they liked it or not." Mac laughed and looked over at Sedona. "That's Asher and Livi. They're twins, by the way."

"Really? Actually, I can see that."

He nodded. Their hair and eyes were the same colors. They were also the same height until they hit puberty, and Asher shot up, passing Livi by eight inches. "Do you guys rent the van for tours? I imagine it's way cheaper than a bus."

"It would be much cheaper," Lou confirmed. "Even with paying for hotels. Those buses cost an arm and a leg."

"Actually, the van and trailer were a gift from my grand-mother." A smile brightened Sedona's face. "She said she wished she could come along, and the best she could do was make sure we had a safe vehicle to drive."

"Wow, that was an extremely thoughtful gift." And expen-sive. It was also practical. At least, with a new vehicle, there were fewer issues with it just breaking down.

They rode the rest of the way to the auditorium on campus. Nick got them around to the back entrance, where he parked the van and trailer as close as possible. Mac pointed out the parking lot security cameras, and they made sure to park where most of the van and trailer could be seen should they have a problem with vandalism or anyone trying to tape notes to the vehicles.

They had two hours to get everything unloaded and the

equipment set up before the concert began. Mac helped get things inside, but he made sure he wasn't too overloaded, and that he stuck close to Sedona the whole time.

He couldn't help but notice that Connor did very little to help with the equipment. To his credit, though, he did stay close to Sedona.

Tickets had been sold ahead of time, but were available for people walking in. It would be impossible to prepare for how many people would be in attendance. Mac might not be able to be on stage with Sedona, but he hoped to be nearby, where he could see what was going on.

There were dressing rooms for the men and women to use. Mac made sure the women's dressing room was secure before Sedona and Chloe disappeared inside to change. He waited beside the door to make sure they weren't disturbed.

He was wholly unprepared for the vision that stepped out. His attention was immediately drawn to Sedona.

Her dress, a velvet-like material in a beautiful sapphire blue, fit her perfectly and hung just below her calves. The skirt flowed around her as she walked. Her hair, wavy and soft, fell to the middle of her back and framed her face. The color of the dress made her pretty eyes pop.

The first word that entered Mac's head was "graceful" as she and Chloe chatted back and forth. Sedona had the kind of poise that he imagined a finishing school would be proud of. Looking at her now, you'd never know the kind of stress she was under. Instead, she looked excited as she talked animatedly, and her eyes sparkled with a joy that was impossible to ignore.

It took some effort on his part to stop staring at her before she noticed. He was there to keep her safe. He absolutely refused to be one more person who made her feel uncomfortable.

Lou had already performed his sound check. All they had

to do now was wait until it was time for the performance to begin.

Twenty minutes later, he stood behind the scenes on the right side of the stage and watched as Sedona and the band got into their places. The stage held all their equipment while still giving the impression that they might as well be singing in someone's living room. There was even a Christmas tree in one corner and an electric fireplace with a chimney that looked real nearby.

As soon as Sedona began to sing, it was clear that the stage was exactly where she was meant to be. Her lovely voice filled the auditorium with its smooth, rich tone that he didn't think he'd ever forget. No wonder the auditorium was nearly filled with an audience that was hanging onto her every word.

Sedona had a way of engaging the audience, too. She glided around the stage like she owned it, walking near the edge and singing to the people in the first couple of rows. Several times, she reached out to touch the hands of those who were reaching up to her.

Every time she stepped up to the edge of the stage like that, Mac couldn't help but tense. He tried to dismiss that feeling, but it was insistent. Finally, he looked across the stage to where Connor was stationed on the opposite side. He caught Connor's eye, then motioned to himself and then the floor in front of the stage. Connor nodded his agreement.

Mac went behind the stage and around then came in the door at floor level. Everyone was focused on Sedona and the members of the band, allowing him to casually walk to the set of stairs that led from the floor to the stage. He took up his position there and continued to watch the performance.

Sedona's song ended, and she looked out over the crowd. Her gaze passed over him momentarily, letting him know that she'd seen his change in position.

"It's been amazing being here with you all tonight. Can you believe we have less than three weeks until Christmas?"

The crowd cheered, and Sedona flashed a bright smile that lit up her whole face.

"What do you say to an old-fashioned Christmas sing-along before we go tonight?"

Again, there was more cheering as Nick and Joel disappeared offstage and returned with a plush, off-white chair that they carried to the front and middle of the stage.

Sedona held her skirt as she sat, crossed her ankles, and then accepted the acoustic guitar that Chloe handed to her.

So far tonight, Mac had heard her sing, but this was the first time he was going to hear her play. He watched in awe as her hands moved effortlessly across the guitar strings, ushering in the opening melody of "Angels We Have Heard on High." The other instruments began to accompany her. Soon, Sedona's beautiful voice was joined by the audience as music glorifying the birth of Jesus filled the air.

Most of the people listening joined in, and Mac found himself doing the same.

The fact that she was sitting on the chair, relaxing with everyone, made the whole experience feel special like they were all a part of the concert instead of just sitting there watching it.

The songs built up to "We Wish You a Merry Christmas," and as she started to sing, she stood and walked closer to the edge of the stage. The audience sang along with her.

Out of the corner of his eye, Mac saw one of the men in the front row approach the stage. Before he could even respond, the man reached out and snagged Sedona's ankle with his hand.

Somehow, she managed to lift her foot up and out of her slipper-like shoe without falling, although she did stumble back as she regained her balance.

Mac was already there when the man turned around, lifted the shoe above his head, and cheered.

He grabbed the man by the arms and twisted them behind his back, making him drop the shoe as he protested loudly. Without a word, Mac marched the man across the floor to the exit, where Connor was waiting.

Connor took over holding the man's arms.

"Take him out and make sure the police are called. Assault and battery charges can be filed." Mac motioned to the stage behind him. "I'll stay here and keep an eye on Sedona for the remainder of the concert."

"You've got it." Connor pushed the man toward the exit. "Come on," he growled as they exited the auditorium.

Adrenaline had Mac's heart thudding as he turned and strode back to his original position, stooping to retrieve Sedona's shoe along the way. Two different people congratulated him on his quick response, to which he gave a nod of thanks.

On stage, Sedona had removed her other shoe and was just finishing the song. The audience gave her a standing ovation.

Sedona smiled brightly as she was joined at the front of the stage by the rest of the band. She waved and looked out over the crowd, but her gaze settled on Mac for a moment as she mouthed, "Thank you."

He gave her an encouraging nod, and his impression of her increased significantly. The fact that she was able to go through someone grabbing her like that and keep singing was a testament to her strength. He couldn't bring himself to smile, though. What he wanted was to talk to her and make sure she was okay.

Because that guy should never have had the opportunity to reach Sedona in the first place, and he was going to make sure nothing like that happened again.

ELEVEN

What was even more amazing than the concert itself was how the audience really seemed to enjoy the interaction. The more they sang along with the Christmas carols at the end, the more Sedona loved every minute of it. Until that guy had reached out and grabbed her foot. Even now, she wasn't sure how she managed to keep her balance while holding her guitar.

She was still amazed at how quickly Mac stepped in to handle the situation. Dressed in a pair of jeans, a green, long-sleeved shirt, and a black jacket, he'd blended in with the crowd. Exactly what he'd wanted. But when trouble appeared, he didn't miss a beat.

Even now, she could feel his gaze on her as she and her bandmates gave the crowd one last wave and headed off stage.

Chloe put an arm around her. "I'm so glad you're okay. That was freaky. What was that guy thinking?"

"I don't know." Sedona leaned her head against her friend's.

"It definitely could've been worse," Joel told them as he moved to Sedona's other side.

Mac bounded up the stairs, snatched her other shoe from the floor, and followed them backstage.

They'd barely made it past the curtain when he cupped her elbow. "Are you okay?" He gently led her to a folding chair and urged her to sit down. "Did he hurt you?"

"I'm okay." She handed her guitar to Chloe and looked down at her left foot. She twisted it slightly so she could see her ankle, which had been a little sore since the incident. To her surprise, three red lines led from the middle of her calf all the way down to her ankle, no doubt caused by the creep's fingernails.

Mac immediately lifted her foot to examine the damage. "He didn't break the skin." His voice was tight and his shoulders rigid. "Thank God for that."

She was about to echo his sentiment when he gently tugged her shoes back onto her feet. There was no doubt he was simply being kind, but the gesture felt somehow intimate, and the very fact that she even thought that sent warmth to her cheeks.

With a prayer that no one noticed, she quickly got to her feet, and he stood along with her. "Really, I'm okay. Thank you for reacting so quickly. I never imagined someone would try to do something like that."

Sedona shivered and already made plans to stand farther back from the edge of the stage from then on. If she'd fallen, she could've ended up hurt or with a broken guitar. At the very least, it would've been mortifying.

She sent a silent prayer heavenward. *Thank you, Father, for keeping me safe.*

"Connor is with the guy and should've called the police by now. We'll both need to give our statements so you can press charges for assault and battery."

Her eyes widened. "Do you think this is the guy who's been after me? The stalker?"

"No, I don't. I think he was a dumb kid who probably

acted on a dare. However, we need to be sure." With that, he took out his phone and sent a text. A moment later, one came back. "Connor says the police are here and waiting for us."

Sedona had more questions, but with everyone bustling about, now wasn't the time. If it was just a kid who did something stupid like Mac thought, she almost hated the idea of pressing charges. Especially if it meant having to stay in Destiny longer than they'd planned. They really needed to head to Austin first thing tomorrow morning.

Nick moved forward. "We've got everything handled here." He placed a hand on Sedona's shoulder and leaned in, his face almost uncomfortably close. "You guys should meet the police. See what's going on."

She took a step backward.

"Agreed," Joel said as he passed them. "We'll come find you once we have everything packed up."

"Thank you." She looked over and up at Mac. "Lead the way."

Sedona was wholly unprepared to find herself face-to-face with a kid who couldn't have been older than twenty. To his credit, he looked incredibly embarrassed now that he was no longer holding up the trophy of her shoe in front of his friends.

Once they'd entered the room, Connor went back to help the crew and keep an eye on everyone else. That left Mac and Sedona in the room with the kid, whose name was Ricky, and two Destiny Police Officers.

"You understand that you could be charged for assault and battery, don't you?" The officer with the name Carrington on his uniform pulled a chair out and sat in front of Ricky.

"For stealing the lady's shoe? Really?" The young man stared at Officer Carrington and then turned his attention to Sedona. "Look, I'm sorry. It was stupid."

Mac was standing next to Sedona, but she got the sense that he would've loved to say a thing or two himself.

The female officer, Patterson, according to her name badge, gave him an incredulous look. "Ms. Reeves could've fallen off the stage or tripped and hurt herself. You're incredibly lucky that all she sustained were a few scratches tonight."

The kid leaned forward to rest his elbows on his knees and ran his hands over his face. Finally, he lowered them again and looked Sedona right in the eyes. "I'm sorry. Truly. I can promise you I'll never do something stupid like that again."

"I appreciate the apology." Sedona, suddenly cold, folded her arms across her chest. "And I sincerely hope that's true."

Mac shifted his feet and addressed Officer Carrington. "May we speak with you outside, please?"

"Of course." He nodded to Officer Patterson, who remained with Ricky. Once in the hallway, the door was closed again. "What else can I do for you, Mac?"

Interesting, so apparently Mac had met the officer before. Then again, he had commented on working with local law enforcement should the need arise. Apparently, they already had a working relationship.

Mac explained to the officer about her situation with the stalker, including the peeping tom at the hotel and the whispered threat the night before. "I don't believe Ricky is the one responsible, but I'd appreciate it if your office would keep that in mind when you charge him. More importantly, I'm hoping this is enough to open an investigation here in Destiny. Asher has quite a bit of information that he'd be happy to forward to you, and I know he could use some help from Logan to run down a few leads."

"Absolutely. Our department will do everything it can to help." Officer Carrington offered Sedona a charming smile. "I'm sorry for the trouble you've been having Miss Reeves, but you're in good hands. I'll let you know as soon as I have more information on Ricky. In the meantime, I think I've gotten everything from you two that I need. You're free to go." He ducked back inside the office, leaving Mac and Sedona in the hallway alone.

Suddenly exhausted and still cold, she released a heavy sigh.

"Are you sure you're okay?" Mac shrugged off his jacket and draped it over her shoulders, his warmth immediately helping to ward off the chill.

She used one hand to hold it closed in front of her. "Thank you. And yes, I'm fine. Honestly, it's a real good thing I don't drink."

"Neither do I. So, what is your vice? You know, what you do when you're stressed or need to wind down? I mean, everyone's got one, right?"

She hesitated. "Ice cream. Specifically, cookies and cream. I usually have pints of it in my freezer when I'm home. What about you?"

"I work out at the gym when I'm frustrated or need to blow off some steam. But I never say no to ice cream, either. Especially if rocky road is on the table."

Sedona's eyes darted to his arms which, now that he was no longer wearing his jacket, were clear evidence of his time spent lifting weights.

If Mac noticed, he was graceful enough to pretend like he hadn't. "Maybe we should stop on the way back to the hotel and get some ice cream. There's a great place that's open late right down the street." He nodded toward her feet. "Do you need to change before we leave?"

"Yes, changing would be good. Then I can give you your coat back."

"You can keep it for as long as you need it. Let's go find the others and see where we're at with packing everything up."

They'd finished a short while ago and had been waiting in the main lobby for the two of them to return. Chloe carried a bag with Sedona's change of clothes. Mac double checked the changing room for them before they went in.

"Thanks for getting my things." Sedona reached for the bag and disappeared into one of the changing stalls. The first thing she did was take off Mac's jacket and hang it on a hook. She immediately missed the warmth, although she could still smell the faint hints of leather and pine that it left behind. "Are you up for ice cream or something to eat?"

"Are you kidding? I'm starving. The guys are, too."

"Awesome." Sedona stepped out of the dress and quickly put on a cozy brown sweater and a pair of comfortable jeans. "I'm not in a huge hurry to get back to the hotel. I've gotta say, I'm glad Mac and Lou got most of our hotel rooms swapped to the second or third floors for the rest of the tour."

Chloe's voice almost echoed since they were the only two in the room. "Hiring Mac was the right thing to do. I'm sure glad he was there tonight."

"Me, too." She pulled on a pair of wool socks, which were normally soft and comforting, but tonight they irritated the scratches on her leg.

Once again, she was reminded of how much worse things could have been. Would her stalker hesitate to cause her physical harm if he had the opportunity? The possibility sent chills down her spine.

TWELVE

The blinker ticked as Nick waited for space to open up so he could merge into the next lane. "Destiny was a nice break from the big city mess. I'm already not a fan of Austin traffic," he muttered under his breath.

Thankfully, someone was kind enough to allow him enough space to merge the van and trailer over.

Sedona agreed with Nick wholeheartedly. She'd grown up in Houston, and she lived in Dallas now. While she was certainly used to the large cities, she didn't enjoy driving in them. The sheer amount of traffic was stressful, not to mention it took way longer to get from one side of town to the other than it ought to. A smaller town like Destiny was much easier to get around.

She yawned and looked out her window as the towering buildings in the distance grew larger.

Even though she slept okay last night, especially with the door wedge in place and a security camera in her hotel window, she was still exhausted. She'd tried to sleep on the way, but her mind kept spinning in circles. She needed to be careful not to get too worn out. If she got sick and it affected her voice, the tour was over.

They only had one concert here tonight, and then tomorrow they could take their time since they weren't leaving for Houston until two in the afternoon. Sedona decided then and there to make a point of relaxing and getting a little extra sleep. After all, it wouldn't kill her if she didn't go down for breakfast first thing tomorrow morning.

Tonight's concert was at an outdoor community stage with the potential for quite the crowd, especially considering they were opening for a much larger group.

Just thinking about it made Sedona's stomach tighten with excitement and nerves. Would performing in front of others ever become second nature? Part of her hoped that it would. Yet, she never wanted to take this kind of experience for granted. Not for the first time, she thanked God for making her dream come true.

Nick mumbled again as he continued to follow the van's GPS.

Joel spoke up from the third row. "You think this is bad, wait till we get to Houston."

"I don't even want to think about it."

An hour later, they pulled into the hotel parking lot. Joel and Lou went inside to check in.

Connor rolled down his window and stuck his head out to look up at the building that towered above them. "What floor did Lou say he got our rooms moved to? I hope it wasn't anywhere near the top. You can actually feel the building move when you're up that high."

"We're on the third. No risk of a peeping tom trying to look through the window, but we shouldn't be rocked to sleep either." Mac chuckled. "We aren't any higher than the third floor, no matter where we go after this."

"Thank goodness for that," Connor muttered under his breath.

Chloe gave a quiet laugh from behind them, and Sedona took her seat belt off and turned so she could see her friend.

As soon as they locked eyes, they were both struggling to hold their laughter. The fact that the poor man was scared of heights shouldn't be funny, but Connor was so serious most of the time.

If he realized they were laughing at him, he made no indication.

Sedona pressed her hand to her mouth and had to avert her eyes from Chloe's to stop the giggles. She caught Mac's amused expression, his eyes shining, as Joel and Nick returned.

Twenty minutes later, they'd parked in view of the security cameras on the side of the hotel where the van and trailer could be seen from most of their hotel rooms. Mac also said he'd set up one of the portable security cameras in his window to record the vehicles overnight.

Now Sedona was alone in her hotel room, and after being in the van with everyone for nearly five hours, the quiet was wonderful. Especially since they'd need to leave for the venue in a couple of hours to make sure they got everything set up.

She paced to the window and looked out. At least she wouldn't have to worry about some creep trying to look in. Between that and the wedge to put against her door, hopefully, tonight would be much more restful.

Her phone rang, and she cringed when she saw her mother's name. With a fortified breath, she answered the call. "Hey, Mom. How are you and Dad doing?"

"Oh, we're fine. Are you in Austin yet?"

Sedona rolled her eyes. No doubt Connor had messaged them and told them that very thing earlier. "Yes, we're settled in the hotel and getting ready for the concert tonight."

"That's nice."

A long, dramatic pause followed that Sedona recognized as her cue to tell them something new.

"We had a little trouble in Destiny, so I hired a second man for private security. I think he and Connor will have everything under control. We have the one concert here, and then we'll be on our way to Houston tomorrow."

Where her parents lived. They hadn't come to any of her concerts since she went independent, and she didn't expect them to start now.

"Oh, honey." Mom's words dripped with fabricated sorrow. "Dad and I so wish we could be there. But he's been called away on business, and I'm with him now. We figured, since we had to go to Rome anyway, we might as well make a mini vacation out of it. We'll be back in town on Tuesday."

Someone knocked on Sedona's door. She looked through the peephole to see Mac standing on the other side. She unlocked the door and ushered him in.

"We'll be in San Antonio by then. But it's fine. I hope you and Dad enjoy your mini vacation." It took all she had to keep her own disappointment from bleeding into her voice. After all, she expected nothing less. Still, she was going to be performing in a large venue in her parents' hometown. Was it really too much to expect them to want to see their only child in her element?

Mac watched her from his spot near the door, concern etched into his features. Apparently, she hadn't been successful at keeping her emotions from showing on her face.

"Thank you. Well, I'd better let you get settled. We've got a dinner party later this afternoon. I need to find somewhere to get my hair done. You stay safe. Love you."

With that, the line went dead before Sedona even had the opportunity to return the sentiment. There was a good chance she wouldn't hear from them again until they'd returned to Houston, unless she made the effort to call them.

"I'm sorry. I didn't mean to intrude. I can come back later." Mac motioned to the door as though he were ready to walk back out if she preferred.

"No, it's okay." She turned away from him and went to retrieve her bottle of water from the side table. Not so much because she was thirsty, but because she needed a moment to push back her emotions. "It was just my mom."

"Your parents live in Houston, right?"

She nodded and took a long drink of her water. When she'd finished, he was watching her expectantly. "Mom was letting me know they wouldn't be at either concert since they're out of town for a business trip and decided to turn it into a mini vacation." She tried to make it sound like she didn't care, but she could tell by his expression that he didn't believe that.

"I'm sorry, Sedona."

"It is what it is." She noticed that he carried an iPad under his arm. "Is everything okay?"

"Oh. Yes." He grasped the iPad and held it up. "Asher was hoping to squeeze in a conference call and give us some updates. Are you feeling up to it?"

"Definitely. Did he give you any idea of what they might have found out?"

"Not really, though I understand he's been working with Logan Alcott at the Destiny Police Department. Logan is their tech guy. Between the two of them, if there's information to be found, they'll locate it."

Sedona took in her surroundings, noticing how compact the hotel room was—easily the smallest she'd ever booked. Even so, she preferred it to staying at her parents' place, regardless of whether they were home. Since she'd only be using the room to sleep and shower, she didn't need anything more spacious.

She motioned to the tiny table shoved into the corner of the room. They shifted the two chairs so they were side by side.

Mac set the iPad up and turned it on. Then he sent a text on his phone, presumably to let Asher know they were ready.

A few moments later, a video call came in, and Asher's face appeared on screen.

"Hey, guys. How's it going?"

Sedona gave a friendly wave while Mac replied.

"Good. We're in Austin now and in the hotel. We'll be heading to the venue in a couple of hours. Were you able to find out any more about Ricky from last night?"

"Yep. Been in contact with both Logan and Officer Carrington. They checked his alibi for several of the other incidents, and there's no way this guy's your stalker. He did have alcohol in his system, and it looks like he wasn't exactly at his best when he made a stupid decision. All in all, it was random and unrelated."

It was the news she'd been expecting, but she couldn't help but be a little disappointed. After all, that meant her stalker was still out there. Somewhere.

Had he been watching them as they left Destiny? Did he follow them all the way to Austin? Or did he have a way to find out which hotel they'd reserved and was waiting for her here?

What if she'd passed right by him in the hallway on the way to the elevator?

He could be anyone, anywhere, and she wouldn't even know.

THIRTEEN

Sedona had grown quiet, and there was a pensive look on her face that bordered on apprehension. Mac placed his palm against her upper back. "Hey, eliminating people from the suspect list is progress, too."

She looked over and up at him as though she were trying to absorb some of his reassurance. To his surprise, she leaned in just enough for her upper arm to rest lightly against his. Instead of dropping his hand, he left it against her back as the warmth from her skin seeped through her purple sweater.

"I do have some good news," Asher offered. "I gave Officer Carrington all the information we have on your stalker so far and emphasized the events that happened here in Destiny. They've officially opened a case here, which means I'll be able to share any details we get with them and hopefully have additional help when it comes to background checks and things like that."

"Which is a really good thing," Mac gave her an encouraging nod. "Are they able to check for fingerprints on the notes?"

"Yep, they're processing them now. But they've been in a lot of hands, so I don't know what they'll be able to find. We did check into those break-ins at the hotel in Little Rock. According to the police reports, items were stolen from two of the rooms. It could be that they were hit fast and hard, and only high-value items were worth taking. It doesn't seem to be related to the stalker. Have you received any more texts?"

"None." Which was somewhat odd in itself. She'd been getting them regularly for several days. Did he stop because she refused to respond? Did her lack of response make him angry?

Ugh!

She really needed to stop letting her mind go down those scary rabbit holes.

"With your permission, Logan will pull your phone records and see if we can track down the phone used to send those texts. That said, if he's using a burner—and I suspect he is—then there won't be much to go on. Now, if he ever calls you, we can trace that call in real time and see if we can't triangulate his location."

"Yes, of course. Feel free to get any of my information you need."

"Perfect." Asher's attention drifted from the camera to what she guessed was the screen of his laptop. "I'm almost done here. Then I'll let you guys go. I finished my check on Lou and Nick. There isn't much to report on Lou. Other than two parking tickets, he doesn't have any kind of record. Looks like he had a number of jobs through the years, but all were related to media and sound in one way or another. This is one of his longest."

Mac liked Lou. He was a guy who told it like it was, which was something he greatly appreciated. "And what about Nick?"

He wanted to talk to Sedona about the way Nick had been in her face after the incident last night, but they never really got the chance.

"It turns out that Nick does have a record. Not a long one,

and nothing new in the last ten years." Asher's brows rose as he looked over his notes. "Two separate times in college, he was accused of physical abuse toward a girlfriend. These incidents were almost three years apart. Both women filed for a restraining order but eventually dropped the charges. He was never actually convicted of anything."

Sedona's muscles tensed as she straightened her spine. "Did the reports give any details? And nothing at all since then?"

"No details listed. The only reason I could find anything at all was because of the restraining orders. It seems he's been on the straight and narrow since then, though."

"Or he's really good at covering his tracks." Mac hated dealing with men who hurt women in any capacity.

Livi was assaulted by a man when she was a freshman in college, and she'd never fully recovered. He saw the way she struggled sometimes, and that was especially true when it came to even considering the possibility of getting close to a guy that wasn't a family member. The idea that there might be a predator in the band made him angry.

He slipped his hand from Sedona's back to her shoulder and gave it a squeeze. "I noticed last night that Nick was concerned about Sedona after the concert. He was trying to make her feel better, but he got in her space." He dropped his hand and motioned to her. "Am I right? Or did it not feel that way to you?"

"He was definitely too close. I mean, we work together, and I like the guy, but we're not friends like that." A noticeable shiver coursed through her body. "And now I'm not going to look at him the same. What if both of those allegations were false, and he's perfectly innocent? It's not fair that I'm going to be questioning his motives from now on. Besides, he was playing with us on stage when several of the incidents occurred."

Mac leaned forward in his chair and ran his fingers

through his hair. "Honestly? I think you're probably right. However, I'm not about to gamble your safety on it. He could be working with someone else, too. There are several scenarios. Asher, is it possible for the police to find out more details about the allegations against Nick? Talk to the women who filed the restraining orders?"

"I'll check into it and update you when I find out. Oh, Mac? Dad wants you to call him when you get the chance. He's considering offering Truitt a position with the company and would like your opinion."

"I'll do that. Thanks, Asher."

"You bet. You two be careful, and I'll check in again soon."

With that, the video call ended.

"It's nice you all get to give input when it comes to new hires."

Mac turned off his iPad. "You remember meeting Ivy yesterday at the Castle? Truitt's her brother. He and Gavin met in the Army. Anyway, he just got out and is looking for a change in career, and we thought he'd fit in well with the team. We've been really busy lately, so having an extra hand on deck would be a real help."

"Your family sounds amazing. Seriously, has Hallmark ever contacted you guys about being on the front of some of their Christmas cards?"

Mac laughed loudly. It was obvious she envied his family, and given what he'd heard of hers, he couldn't blame her.

"I love my family, and we're close, but trust me when I say things aren't always perfect, far from it. Every family has their ups and downs. You have to remember that what you see on the outside isn't always the whole story."

She looked doubtful. Mac wasn't going to tell her about Livi's trauma or how the family struggled to help her through it. That was her story to tell. Cole's background, however, was one his half-brother freely shared.

"I mentioned Cole was my half-brother, right?"

She nodded.

"Well, we share a mom. My dad was with a woman named Carol, and they had me. Unfortunately, she had a lot of substance abuse struggles, and their relationship couldn't survive that, so they separated, and I stayed with my dad.

"Carol went on to have multiple relationships, and two years later, Cole was born. Since she and my dad still communicated for my sake, I did get to see Cole on occasion, and he even stayed with us a few times. When Cole was thirteen, she brought him over to our house in the middle of the night, said she couldn't handle it anymore, and asked Dad to take him in. She never came back or reached out again."

Sedona's mouth opened like she was going to say something. Then she closed it again as tears flooded her eyes. "I can't even imagine. Poor Cole. I take it his biological father wasn't in the picture."

"No, he wasn't. Years before that night, Dad met Ruth, whom I consider my mom, and they had four kids together. They offered Cole a home so that he would grow up with a supportive family. I'm thankful their relationship is so strong because Cole really struggled with anger when he first came to live with us. It got better with time, but it wasn't until last year when he met Erica that he was finally able to set aside some of the residual resentment he'd been carrying around."

"So, your parents raised Cole when he wasn't even their own biological child? Wow. That says a lot about them both."

"Yeah, it does, and the fact that we all rallied around our dad while he was fighting cancer was a way we could show them just how much that meant. Praise God, he's in remission now. When you see a fortified castle on the outside, you can't truly know the struggles, sacrifices, and care that went into placing each brick. All families are like that—whether formed by blood or by choice. It takes effort and dedication to hold everything together."

"I'd never thought about it that way. At least I grew up

with a warm place to live, food, and two parents. I could've had worse." There was a hint of guilt in her voice. "From the outside, my household and family looked perfect, too. But I'm pretty sure that, if a wave hit it, everyone would have seen our castle was only made of sand."

"You have no reason to feel bad, Sedona. You deserved to be raised by parents who made you feel wanted and loved. You have every right to wish things had been different. I just didn't want you to think that my family was perfect either. I know what it's like to wonder why things have to be the way they are."

Mac couldn't help comparing his failed relationship in the past to what his parents had, what Cole found with Erica, and even the connection Gavin had with Ivy. He'd come to the realization that that kind of love might not have been in the cards for him, and it was better to treasure the relationships he did have. That worked—most of the time.

And then a pretty blonde hired him to protect her, and after only spending a couple of days with her, he was already sad to know they'd be going their separate ways sooner rather than later. It was a fact he barely acknowledged to himself and had no plans of admitting to anyone else, including Sedona.

FOURTEEN

The concert was at an outdoor venue, and even in her black jeans and red knit sweater tunic, Sedona was absolutely freezing. She finally put on her black coat that she planned to wear until the last minute. Sadly, she'd already gotten chilled by then, and while the coat offered protection against the wind, she couldn't seem to get warmed up again.

They still had an hour before their performance even started. She just hoped and prayed that she'd be able to keep the shivers racking her body from showing up in her voice. There was a roof over the stage where they would be performing, but that didn't mean much with the cold wind whipping through the open space.

Lou glanced up from the soundboard he was working on and gave her an apologetic look. They didn't have to say a word to come to the agreement that, if they ever did another tour in the late fall or early winter, all venues would be indoors.

"So what exactly is Lou doing now?" Mac had his hands tucked into the pockets of his heavy coat.

"He's setting up our IEMs." She tapped her headphones

that plugged into a bodypack clipped at her waist. "Every time we come to a new venue, he has to scan the radio airwaves to look for clear frequencies, assign those frequencies to each of us, and then sync that frequency to our bodypacks."

"And what do you hear through your headphones? Do you all hear the same things?"

"Not necessarily." Sedona led the way to the mixer where Lou was working, and Mac followed. "Each of us gets a custom-tailored mix of the music. Most importantly, though, it makes it easier to hear myself and the rest of the band. Otherwise, the stage itself can be so loud that it's easy to get lost."

"I had no idea." Mac watched Lou and asked several more questions. Lou seemed to appreciate the interest and had no problem explaining what he was doing. "It seems like it could get confusing sometimes."

Lou shrugged. "Maybe when you're first learning. It's not a big deal at all anymore."

Once they had everything set up and had tested the sound, they all got to escape inside a large area reserved for bands and the like, where they could wait in the warmth until it was time to take the stage.

Sedona blew on the palms of her hands and rubbed them together. The owners of the venue had set out warm drinks of all kinds along one wall, and most of the band moved off to choose one to enjoy while they waited.

She was about to do that, too, when Mac stepped in front of her.

"Will you do me a favor tonight?" His gaze snagged hers, and he looked serious.

"Sure. What is it?"

"Stay at least an arm's length away from the edge of the stage at all times." A ghost of a smile tugged at the corners of his mouth, and she laughed.

"Yeah, I can definitely do that."

"Good."

Chloe handed Sedona a cup. "Tea with honey. Figured you might need it tonight."

"Definitely. Thank you." She took a tentative sip and savored the way the herbal tea and honey coated her throat. A glance at the clock told her they were getting close to the time they needed to head back out. And she was just starting to get warmed up.

Her cell phone pinged with a text, reminding her to silence it before the concert. She pulled it out and swiped to unlock her phone and nearly dropped her cup of tea.

"Mac. It's him."

He was instantly on alert as she turned the phone to show him the text.

> I told you I could get to you no matter where you are. Don't freeze those pretty little fingers off.

Mac immediately dialed a number on his own phone. "Hey, Asher. The stalker just texted Sedona again. The text suggests he may be in the immediate vicinity… Will do." He hung up again. He glanced around, probably taking stock of who was in the room with them.

Sedona had done the same thing. Nick was still lingering by the table with the drinks and talking to someone from the band that would be playing after them.

Her hands were shaking, and this time it wasn't from the cold. She took another sip of her drink and dropped the cup into the trash before it slipped from her hands completely.

"Do not let him get into your head." Chloe reached out and pulled Sedona into a hug. "He knows we're here in Austin because your website has the tour schedule. And it doesn't take a genius to check the weather on the internet. That doesn't mean he's here."

87

Sedona nodded and tried to convince herself that Chloe's words were true. It wasn't working, though. He was here somewhere—she could practically feel it.

Suddenly, it felt like the walls were closing in around her as she tried to force her lungs to work. "I need some fresh air."

With that, she pushed past Chloe and headed for the door. She barely registered Mac telling her friend that he had it handled. The moment she was back outside, and the cold air burned her throat, her head started to clear again. She gulped in a breath, and then another.

Mac came into her field of view. He placed his hands on her shoulders and bent down enough to look into her face. "Just focus on one breath at a time. In. Out."

She instinctively leaned her forehead against his chest and nodded as she struggled to slow her breathing. Mac stood still as a statue for a moment before his hands left her shoulders, and he wrapped his arms around her and pulled her close.

"You've got this. We're not going to let anything happen to you. *I'm* not going to let anything happen to you."

She focused on his words, spoken near her ear, and the way his warmth seemed to envelope her. Not only did the cold seem to fade away, but for the first time in days—maybe weeks—she felt completely safe.

The tension in her shoulders eased, and her breaths came easier.

"There you go." Mac took a step back, and his arms released her, allowing the cold air to rush in between them. "I've already spoken with Connor. He's going to be down on the ground at the front of the stage. I'll be up on top so I can get a clearer view of what's going on. I've also communicated with local security and let them know you've been having some trouble, so we'll have extra eyes on the place tonight."

"Yeah. That's good." Sedona kept her gaze on the front of his jacket, where she had been nestled against him just moments before. Embarrassment over leaning into him like that flooded through her. "I'm sorry, that was way out of line—"

"You've done nothing to be sorry for." He moved his arm like he was going to reach out to her but seemed to change his mind and put his hand in the jacket pocket instead. "I'm going to be within view the whole time."

Sounds of shuffling and footsteps came up behind them, and she turned to find the rest of her bandmates exiting the building. It was showtime, and Sedona seriously needed to pull it together.

Together, they all made the trek back to the stage, made their final preparations, and then stepped out onto the wooden plattorm to the applause of a large crowd.

Sedona focused on them as they began their first set. All of these people had braved the horribly cold weather to come out and listen to them sing, and she wasn't about to let them down. As her fingers flew over her guitar and her voice rose, she looked to her right to find Mac watching her from the side. He gave her a nod of respect that meant as much to her as anything he could've said.

When the final song was over, they took a bow and waved to thank the audience for coming out. Sedona had just turned to walk off stage when a voice spoke over the headphones, the voice booming in her ears and sending a wave of panic through her chest.

"Enjoy the applause, Sedona. It won't last forever."

FIFTEEN

"How is that even possible? I mean, could he just hijack any of our IEMs whenever he wants and start talking to us? That's seriously messed up." Chloe's voice had risen an octave as she settled in the van and yanked the zipper of her jacket down.

They'd had very little time to talk about the situation because another group was going up on stage. They had to pack all their instruments and equipment back into the trailer to clear out the space.

Lou spoke up from the third row of the van. "It's not hard to intercept the radio frequency we were using for Sedona's IEM. It might have taken a while, but with dedication and a tool that's easy to find, it would then be a simple matter of broadcasting his own message to her headphones. Unfortunately, there's not much we can do to prevent that again in the future."

Mac looked back at him. The man, who seemed naturally serious, looked more than a little frustrated. "They've got security cameras running all over the place. I spoke with the manager, and they're going to send footage within thirty minutes of each side of that message over to Asher who'll forward it on to the Destiny Police Department. The problem is, we don't even know what we're looking for. Lou, how close would someone have to be to intercept the radio frequency?"

"IEMs transmit a low-power, short-range signal. He had to have been there in the audience or really close to that area to be able to pull this off."

Which meant he had been able to see Sedona the whole time and probably got a thrill when his voice in her ear shook her.

That thought made Mac even angrier. He would do everything in his power to make sure no one laid a hand on her. But this kind of harassment? How was he supposed to protect her from that?

Back at the venue, he'd been worried she was having a panic attack when she left the break area. He'd watched his parents help Livi through several in the past, so he thought he might be able to help Sedona refocus.

He never expected her to wind up wrapped in his arms. While she was struggling to catch her breath, all he could think about was shielding her from anything that might harm her. The problem was hat, in that moment, the thought instinctively extended beyond the tour, certainly well past the point where he'd be hired to do so.

The attraction he'd felt toward her the moment they met was morphing into something stronger, and Mac wasn't willing to examine it further. He was responsible for keeping her safe, and he would *not* allow his emotions to cloud his judgment.

The fact was, they were on very different paths in life. When this tour ended, she'd move on, and he'd go back to Destiny. He knew the devastation of watching the woman he loved walk away. He refused to even set himself up for that possibility again.

Connor sat up straight to look at them in the rearview

mirror as Nick drove them back to their hotel. "I kept my eyes on the audience the whole time, and I never saw anyone suspicious. But there had to be, what? Six hundred people there? It'd be easy to hide in a crowd that big."

Mac nodded his agreement. "All we can do is hope that the security cameras caught someone who was obviously not there to enjoy the concert." The odds of that weren't good.

He hadn't said anything out loud, but what the stalker said to Sedona concerned him greatly. All the other notes and texts could be interpreted as someone who was obsessed with her, but possibly from the angle of thinking he was in love with her.

The envelope that was handed to her directly took things a step further. That message tonight was a threat, pure and simple. Things were escalating.

He looked over at Sedona, who hadn't said a word since they all loaded into the van. She was leaning against the side and staring out the window.

Chloe reached forward and put a reassuring hand on her shoulder. "Is there any way we can record messages coming into the IEMs in case it happens again?"

"Unfortunately, that's impossible," Lou replied.

"It's like a one-way street," Joel elaborated. "The message is broadcast to the headphones, but there's nothing being sent from the headphones themselves back to the soundboard to be recorded."

Mac frowned. "But a message could have been pre-recorded and then sent to her IEM, right?"

"Yep."

So the actual stalker didn't even have to be in the crowd as long as he had someone there to broadcast the message. It truly could've been anyone.

The whole situation was maddening.

Mac had asked her earlier whether she recognized the voice and if there was anything distinctive about it. She said it didn't sound familiar, but that it had a slight robotic sound to it. Most likely, the stalker had used some kind of device to change the sound of his voice, making it difficult to match, even if they had gotten a recording of it.

Silence filled the van until Nick glanced at the rearview mirror. "Sedona? Do you need something to eat? It might do you some good to get some food."

"Thanks, Nick. I'm not hungry. But please stop and get something for everyone else."

More silence until Joel finally spoke again from his seat. "Let's grab some burgers on the way back. Once we get to our rooms, I'm sure we're all going to feel like eating before we turn in for the night."

The mood in the van was a far cry from the excited energy that Mac had witnessed after the concert in Destiny. Even after Sedona's foot was grabbed, the day had at least ended with everyone smiling and satisfied with how the performance went overall.

This felt a lot like defeat.

He hated that for everyone, but especially Sedona.

They got dinner and headed back to the hotel. They were all tired and decided to take their food to their own rooms.

Except for Chloe. She put an arm around Sedona. "I don't think you should be eating alone." She motioned to herself and Mac. "Why don't we come in, eat dinner with you, then we'll let you get some rest. I'm worried about you."

Sedona was clearly trying to find a polite way to decline, but Chloe's exaggerated pout, complete with the quivering lip, coaxed a reluctant smile.

"Fine." She gave her friend a playful shove. "You're so bossy."

"Sometimes I've gotta be." She winked at Mac.

He followed the ladies in and locked the door behind them. He sat on the side of the bed to eat so they could sit more comfortably at the little table.

Conversation centered around the cold weather and how, if it was going to be that cold, the least it could do was snow.

"I'm not a fan of snow unless it's Christmas Eve or Christmas Day," Chloe declared as she dragged a fry through her ketchup.

"I love the snow. The whole world gets quieter when the ground is covered with it." Sedona ate several bites of her burger earlier but seemed to have since abandoned it. "I sometimes joke with Grandma that she and I should move to a place with snowy winters. There's just something about that first whiff…"

Chloe laughed out loud then. "All righty, Lorelai Gilmore. Just talking about the white stuff is making me cold again, and I wasn't sure I'd ever feel warm after tonight. Seriously, my fingers were working off pure muscle memory because I couldn't feel them."

"Oh my goodness. I know what you mean." Sedona glanced at Mac with a smile. "Mac asked me to stay away from the edge of the stage—"

"As well you should," Chloe said with a stern look.

"—but my feet were frozen. I don't think I could've walked there if I had to."

The ladies laughed together, and it brought a grin to Mac's face. Chloe knew her friend needed this, and it made his heart lighter to see them both set the stress aside, even if just for the rest of the evening.

He'd finished his food and thought they might like some time just the two of them. Maybe Sedona would talk to Chloe about what happened.

He stood. "I think I'm going to head to my room. If you need anything, Sedona, text or call. I'll see you guys at seven."

They'd all discussed it and decided to meet for breakfast at seven and then head for Houston right away. They were all ready to put Austin in their rearview mirror this trip. Besides, everyone could use an entire day where they didn't have to worry about concerts or anything else.

Chloe wished him good night and then commented about how she hoped she could be up and going without being too much of a zombie.

Sedona walked him to the door, and her blue eyes sought his face. "Thanks, Mac. For everything."

A section of her hair hung down in front of her ear, and Mac had the intense need to brush it back and tuck it behind her ear.

Instead, he reached for the doorknob.

"Of course. Get some rest, okay?"

"Yeah. You, too."

With a final nod, he left and went to his room as soon as he heard her locks slide into place.

Getting some rest himself would be good. Maybe it'd clear his head a little. He couldn't afford to be distracted.

SIXTEEN

Sedona stared at her friend as though she'd just grown a carrot in place of her nose. "You can't be serious. I think that cold weather froze more than just your fingers." She crumpled the fast-food papers and threw them into the trash can situated on the floor next to the dresser.

"I'm dead serious. He likes you, and you'd be crazy if you didn't take one look at that man and not give him a chance." Chloe waggled her eyebrows in a ridiculous fashion. She'd barely waited long enough for Mac to leave the room and the door to close before she'd grinned and revealed her crazy theory.

"He's being paid to hang around me and keep me safe. I think you're making a monumental jump between that and what you're suggesting." She made herself busy unpacking her pajamas and toiletries.

Inside, however, there was a part of her that wanted to squeal like a teenage girl. That likely misplaced assumption of Chloe's sparked way more hope in Sedona's heart than it should have.

Then practicality squashed that hope like a bug.

For one thing, her friend might be imagining things. Not

to mention the man had a job—which he was very good at—in a town where Sedona didn't even live. He had a wonderful family and a stable life. There was no way he'd be looking to change any of that.

Especially considering her schedule wasn't always predictable. She'd need to travel regularly for tours if she wanted to do things right by her career.

Their lives were nearly incompatible.

Despite all that, there was no denying the fact that her heart was drawn to him. Not that she was going to admit that to Chloe, because nothing was going to come of it anyway.

Mac was so kind and always managed to lift her spirits, even when everything around her seemed to be unraveling. Earlier that night, being in his arms—despite her embarrassment—gave her a sense of security she hadn't experienced in a long time. Sedona might not know him well, but she had no doubt that he was someone she'd be proud to call a friend, much less anything more.

Sedona nearly groaned aloud with frustration. Why couldn't she simply push Mac out of her head? It'd be a whole lot easier, that's for sure.

When she finished unpacking her things, she turned to find Chloe looking at her, hands on her hips. "You might be able to fool a lot of people, but you can't fool me. I realize it's complicated. I'm just trying to get you to keep an open mind."

"I hear you, and I appreciate it. Truly." Sedona let herself fall backward onto the bed. "You're going to Galveston, too, right?" It was about an hour and a half away from Houston.

She loved everything about the ocean, and the thought of being this close and not going was practically torture.

Chloe wrinkled her nose. "I will if everyone goes. But it's already cold and will be even more so by the water. I think I'd rather hang around in town and do some shopping."

Sedona did her best to hide her disappointment. "I totally get it. There are so many great stores to walk through."

After all, she might have been the stalker's target, but this was stressful on everyone.

"I'll bet at least one of the guys will want to go, too."

"We'll see." She glanced at the clock sitting on the night-stand. "I'm not trying to rush you, but I need to call Grandma before it gets much later. Then I think I'm going to take a shower and get to bed. I feel like I could sleep for a week."

"It's okay. I'm about ready to call it good for the night, too. Tell your grandma I said hi." Chloe reached down to pull Sedona to her feet, then gave her a hug. "Sleep well."

"Get some rest." She waited for her friend to leave then closed, locked, and blocked the door. She'd barely taken her pajamas and clean clothes into the bathroom when her phone pinged with a text. Expecting it to come from the stalker, she tensed as she tapped on the screen.

To her relief, it was from Mac.

> I'm sorry to bother you, but did you make sure to use the wedge?

His concern for her safety made her smile. She ignored the way her heartbeat picked up speed and responded.

> Yes. The door's locked. Thanks for checking.

> Sleep well.

> You, too.

She thought about sending a moon emoji or something like that and decided against it. Instead, she flopped onto the bed and dialed her grandmother's number.

She told Grandma all about the concerts and how she was

looking forward to going to the beach tomorrow, even if it was winter and would be too cold to wade in the ocean. She also shared how comfortable the van was and that the trailer was working perfectly. There was no way Sedona was going to tell her about the stalker, though. Grandma couldn't do anything about it in Dallas, and everything that could be done was already set in motion.

"I'm looking forward to watching your show when you're back in Dallas. Maybe the next time you go on tour, I can just go right along with you."

Sedona laughed. "Maybe so, Grandma, maybe so. If we don't do that, we need to take some kind of a vacation together. Wouldn't that be fun?"

"Yes, it would. Now, you'd better get some rest and have a safe drive tomorrow. I love you."

"I love you, too, Grandma. I'll check in again in a couple of days before we head for Dallas. Good night."

Listening to her grandmother's sweet voice did her a world of good.

Feeling more relaxed, she plugged her phone in, got a quick shower, then got ready for bed.

Even though her experience in Austin had been less than ideal, at least she didn't have to worry about anyone looking through her hotel room window tonight.

Everyone was tired and dragging the next morning. After a quick breakfast, they checked out and got on the road. Apparently, no one felt much like talking, so they rode most of the way in silence, with the exception of the GPS system giving directions.

Sedona put her earbuds in and continued an audiobook she'd started listening to last week and watched the world go by. It looked like Connor was playing on his phone up front.

She knew Chloe was likely reading, Joel was gaming on his Nintendo Switch, and Lou was probably streaming the church service from home.

Mac was using his iPad and a stylus pen. She couldn't see the screen, but it looked like he was drawing something. He must've noticed her looking because he turned it to face her. She paused her audiobook.

While many details were missing, it was clearly the face of a happy boy.

"This is my nephew, Peter. I thought I'd draw a portrait of him and frame it for my sister-in-law for Christmas."

"Wow, that's impressive. I didn't even know you could use an iPad to draw with that kind of detail." He'd been working on the eyes, which were incredibly life-like. "Did you take art classes?"

"A few in high school, but it was always a hobby of mine. I watch a lot of videos for tips and techniques." He shrugged as if it were no big deal.

Chloe had heard the conversation and was leaning forward in her seat so she could see the screen. "That's amazing, Mac. I'm sure your sister-in-law will love it."

"Agreed. Drawing like that takes a lot of talent." One Sedona definitely didn't have herself.

The tips of his ears turned a light pink as he shrugged again. "Thank you both." With a smile that Sedona would've classified as shy, he went back to work on his portrait.

Chloe gave Sedona a look, then tilted her head toward Mac before grinning and going back to her book.

In another situation, Sedona might've reached back and playfully smacked her friend on the head with a magazine or something. She didn't need Chloe pointing out more reasons why she should like Mac.

She continued her audiobook but had a terrible time paying attention to the narrator and finally just turned it off.

She was about to get a snack out of her bag when Joel set his Nintendo down and leaned forward.

"Does anyone else hear that?"

Mac set his iPad down on his lap, a look of concern on his face.

He leaned forward. "Hey, Nick…"

"Yep, I hear it, too." Nick slowed the van down and put on his right blinker.

That had everyone's attention now.

"What's going on?"

"What's wrong?"

Now that the road noise wasn't as loud, Sedona could hear the odd *thunk-thunk* sound coming from the trailer.

Thankfully, the road had a wide shoulder that they were able to pull over onto and come to a complete stop. Nick waited for several cars to pass before he got out of the van. Connor and Joel joined him.

"Do you think it's a flat tire?" Chloe had taken off her seat belt and was leaning with her arms crossed on the back of the seat between Mac and Sedona. "Do we have a spare?"

"Yes, we have a spare tire for both the van and the trailer," Lou affirmed. "Hopefully, that's all we'll need. I think we're a good forty minutes away from anyplace that can help us otherwise." He frowned as he scrolled on his phone, most likely looking at the maps app.

Sedona groaned. If they needed to buy new tires, it was going to cost a fortune. And what if they were stranded out here until a tow truck arrived? How long would that even take? Selfishly, she'd really been looking forward to going to Galveston to visit the beach this afternoon. There might not be time for that if they had to deal with taking either vehicle in for repairs.

She tried to push away the negative thoughts that were lining up in her mind. Instead, she sent up a silent prayer.

God, please help me to look at the positives here. We're all safe, and whatever's happening, we'll figure it out together.

SEVENTEEN

Mac resisted the urge to get out of the van and see what was going on. He checked the mirrors and didn't see anyone else around, other than the cars that continued to zoom past them on the highway. Still, his place was right here with Sedona, where he could make sure she was safe.

He tucked his iPad into his bag and took off his seat belt so it'd be easier to reach for his firearm if he needed it.

The rear doors of the van opened at the same time Connor climbed back into the passenger seat, his expression grim. "The lug nuts are loose on two of the trailer tires. Nick and Joel are going to tighten those and check the rest of the tires on the trailer and the van. If we hadn't stopped when we did, we would've lost at least one of them."

"Which tires?" Mac already knew the answer before Connor replied to say that they were both on the driver's side.

Sedona looked from him and back to Connor. "What does that mean? Did someone loosen them on purpose?"

Lou spoke up from the seat behind them. "We had the new tires put on the van in Arkansas after they were slashed.

I know they checked all the tires there to make sure they were in good shape. For the lug nuts on one of them to come loose would be rare, but both?"

"That was the side facing away from the hotel, too." Which meant the camera he'd put on his hotel room window to keep an eye on the vehicles likely wouldn't have caught anything. There were only two cameras in the hotel parking lot, but maybe they would get lucky. Mac pulled his phone out and dialed Asher's number. "Hey, someone tampered with the tires on the trailer sometime between the time we got back from the concert and when we left the hotel today. We need security tapes from the hotel parking lot so we can see if they caught anything."

"You got it. You guys okay?"

"We're safe and working on the tires now. Let me know what you find, and I'll text you once we're back on the road."

"Roger that. Be careful."

"Will do. Thanks, Asher."

Chloe spoke up again. "If the lug nuts were loose enough, could the tires have come off completely?"

"Yes, that's exactly what would've happened if we hadn't realized it in time." That might have resulted in major damage to the trailer, not to mention potential loss of equipment inside. It would've put them all in danger, too, depending on the situation.

They all sat in heavy silence until Nick and Joel returned. Nick's face was flushed from exertion as he climbed in behind the steering wheel. "The lug nuts on the van on that side were loose, too."

"Someone definitely did it on purpose then!" Chloe's voice rose in alarm.

Mac clenched his fists and then forced himself to release the tension again. If a wheel had come off the van while they were driving at full speed, they could've all been killed.

"Are we sure it's safe to drive now?" The question came from Sedona, her voice shaky.

"Yes," Nick spoke firmly, and Joel echoed the response. "All lug nuts are tightened, and no permanent damage was done. But from now on, we're going to check the tires before we drive anywhere. Period."

Nick was right. They needed to be much more vigilant.

This had gone from harassment to threats to a direct attempt to physically hurt Sedona and everyone else on the van. The members of the band who were still under suspicion were looking less likely to be the culprit now.

Unless, of course, this was all very controlled. He stared at the back of Nick's head as he carefully pulled the van and trailer onto the highway again.

If Nick were behind everything, he would've known those lug nuts were loose to start with and, as soon as they'd loosened enough to notice, could've pulled over before anything bad happened. It was still a risky game to play.

Trying to find this stalker was like trying to spot shadows in the black of night. What Mac needed was a clear enemy to face off with. Someone he could physically hand over to law enforcement so Sedona would know, without a doubt, that she was free to continue her life without the fear that was haunting her now.

Lou walked away from the hotel counter and started handing key cards out to everyone. He paused in front of Mac, Sedona, and Chloe.

"So, here's the situation. When I originally reserved these rooms, I had a hard time getting so many in the same area. Two of them are connecting rooms. I figured Chloe and Sedona wouldn't mind that, but now, I'm not sure which arrangement y'all would prefer." He looked a little flustered as he handed all three key cards over to Sedona. "I'll let you figure it out."

Apparently, Connor found the whole thing amusing because he didn't even try to hide his chuckle. "I'm going to get my things dropped off and then call the wife."

He'd already spoken to everyone about the fact that he lived in Houston and hadn't seen his wife in almost two weeks outside of video calls. Since Mac would be there, they all agreed it'd be good for Connor to spend some time with his wife, coming back to the hotel to get ready for the performance tomorrow night. The guy practically skipped out of the room and down the hall in anticipation.

Mac still hadn't made up his mind about Connor, and as far as he was concerned, the security guard remained on his suspect list.

Putting that aside, though, he couldn't blame the guy for leaving as soon as possible. If he had a wife he hadn't seen in a while, he'd probably be just as excited.

He turned his attention back to Sedona and Chloe. "After what happened on the road today, and the hijacked IEM last night, I'd prefer to have the connecting room just in case, not that we'll need it. But I will leave the decision up to you." He gave Sedona a nod.

"I think that would be the best choice," Chloe said without giving her friend a chance to respond.

"Then it's settled." Sedona handed each of them a key card. She looked around at their small group. "So, what's the plan? Does everyone want to go to Galveston? There's plenty to do here if anyone would rather stay." She practically bounced on her toes at the thought of their day trip.

Mac had to school his features to keep from smiling because her anticipation of going to the beach was nothing short of adorable.

Nick immediately shook his head. "I'll be honest, I've had

enough driving for today. I think I'm going to stay here, order food in, and be completely lazy."

"I'm with you." Lou held up his key card. "Been to the beach a lot in the past, and I think I'd prefer some downtime and extra sleep."

Chloe nudged Sedona's arm with hers. "You know I'm going. Mostly for the shopping, though. I love all the shops there. It'll be a good time to look for some last-minute Christmas gifts."

"Same. I still need to find something for my mom and sister." Joel took his wallet out and slipped his key card inside. "Neither of them will tell me what they want. We can hit the shops together if you'd like, Chloe."

"Sounds perfect." Chloe beamed. "Maybe we can all meet up for dinner down there somewhere? I'm craving clam chowder."

Mac, of course, would go wherever Sedona went. He had a feeling they'd be spending quite a bit of time on the beach, which meant he needed to dress warmly. It wasn't exactly prime beach season.

With a grin, Sedona pressed her palms together. "Let's all meet back down here in thirty minutes, and we'll head out then."

With that agreed upon, they rode the elevator to the third floor, where their assigned rooms were. Mac asked to check Sedona's for her before he went to his own. She opened the door, and they went inside together.

These rooms were pretty large compared to the ones they had in Austin. In addition to the bed and a small table with chairs, there was also a couch and a coffee table. It was well lit, which Mac always preferred. There was something about a dingy, dark hotel room that made him feel like he was being confined against his will.

"Have you ever stayed in a connected room before?" He pointed to the door that led to his own room.

"No."

"There are two doors that share the same door frame." Mac demonstrated by unlocking the deadbolt, twisting the doorknob, and pulling. The door opened to reveal a second one. "Both are completely independent and have their own locks."

"That's such a great idea. Especially for families traveling together. You could let the kids sleep in one room, the parents in the other, and leave the connecting doors open so it's more like a small apartment."

"Exactly."

She nodded and wandered over to the window. The curtains were already pulled back and the blinds open. They were surrounded by other buildings that were equally as tall as their hotel. The excitement from earlier seemed to drain away in moments.

Mac made sure the window locks were secure, not that they had much to worry about up here. "What is it?"

"Do you think he knows we're staying at this hotel? That I'm in this room?" She shifted away from the window a little. "What if he's in one of those other buildings watching us with a pair of binoculars right now?"

He wanted to tell her there was no way the guy knew where they were, but he refused to lie. Instead, he closed the blinds and curtains, then turned to face her. "If he *is* in one of those other buildings, he can't watch us anymore. In fact, I'll go around and close my blinds, too. Then we'll swap rooms. *If* he's out there, he'll be watching the wrong room anyway."

Her shoulders visibly relaxed, letting him know that she approved of the plan.

"I'll be right back."

He left her room, went into his, closed the blinds, then unlocked his connecting door to find Sedona waiting on the other side. They swapped key cards.

Once they got everything moved to the other room, they

agreed to close the doors but leave them unlocked until they were ready to head back downstairs.

It didn't take long for Mac to pack a small backpack for the excursion. He still had ten minutes to wait when his phone rang. He'd expected a call from Asher, but it was Cole instead.

"Hey, man. Good to hear from you. How are Erica and Peter?"

"Doing well. Both are ready for Christmas break. Hey, I meant to thank you for that suggestion the other day—to pick up some ice cream on the way home. Turned out it was just what she needed."

Mac grinned. "Glad I could help." He may not have been a married man for long— and clearly it was less than successful. He did, however, learn a few things.

"I heard about the lug nuts. I'm glad you guys discovered the problem when you did. The situation definitely sounds like it's escalating."

"Yep. I'm not going to be able to keep an eye on everyone today either." He filled Cole in on the plan for the day. "Sedona is seriously stressed, though, and I think time away from it all will be a good thing. I'm worried about her. I think the reality of how bad this could get hit her today."

"Keep your head on a swivel. If there's any sign at all that you're being followed or in danger…"

"Then we'll call the outing off and get back immediately. No worries, bro. I've got this."

"Well, I was mainly calling to give you a quick update from this end. Forensics at the precinct checked for finger-prints on those notes the stalker sent Sedona. Everything they found belonged to people we expected: the two of us, Chloe, Sedona, Joel, and Connor."

So a dead end, although Mac truly hadn't expected anything different. That was a long shot.

"We also combed through the security footage from the

concert where the IEM was hijacked. They mainly had cameras trained on the stage and a few other key locations. There was no one who stood out."

Mac frowned. "Given our history with this guy, I'm sure he scoped out the cameras ahead of time to make sure he could avoid them."

"Agreed."

If they were still in Destiny, Mac would see if the police could have a guy sit on Connor while another kept an eye on the hotel. Unfortunately, that wasn't something he could arrange here.

A knock came from the connecting door. He opened it again to find Sedona standing there. She'd changed into a peach-colored sweater and had pulled her hair back into a ponytail. Little short strands of hair hung by the sides of her face. A heavy coat was draped over one arm.

"Hey, Cole? I've got to run. We're just about to head back downstairs to meet Joel and Chloe. Call if you find anything. I'll keep you updated on my end."

EIGHTEEN

The Houston skyline disappeared behind them as they drove toward the coast. Mac volunteered to drive the van, having left the trailer in the hotel parking lot, and the rest of them took him up on the offer. Now, Sedona was in the passenger seat. At first, she'd kept glancing at the side mirror to see if any one vehicle kept following them. As traffic thinned out, and it was clear no one was on their tail, she finally started to relax.

"I have no idea what to get my grandfather, though," Chloe was saying. She had been bouncing last-minute gift ideas off Sedona for the past half hour.

"What about one of those nice Hickory Farms sets? You know, the ones with meat, cheese, and crackers? Doesn't everyone love those?"

"I'm a fan," Joel quipped. "Best one I ever tasted was a spicy version. Jalapeño cheese, salsa."

"I never would've thought of that. Granddad does put hot sauce on everything he eats. Okay, Joel, help me keep an eye out for something similar while we're shopping."

"Will do."

Sedona pulled up a map on her phone. They already

decided that, since Joel and Chloe mostly wanted to shop, she and Mac would drop them off at The Strand Historical District, which was near the piers. She found a seafood restaurant in the same vicinity within walking distance. Then they would drive to the beach on the other side of Galveston. "Does that sound good for dinner? We could meet at five, eat, and then head back to the hotel."

Everyone agreed that it sounded great.

Given the high for the day was supposed to be in the mid-sixties, Sedona didn't figure she and Mac would be out by the water all day. Besides, she wouldn't mind the chance to browse the shops a little, too.

She looked over at Mac's profile. He'd commented here and there, but mostly it'd been she and Chloe who had filled the hour-and-a-half drive with chatter. "Thanks again for driving."

He tossed her a smile that warmed her instantly.

"Not a problem. I usually prefer it to riding anyway. We should be getting close."

Sedona turned her focus on the road ahead of them, and when they crossed over Galveston Bay, peace washed over her. She might not have cared if she visited her childhood home in Houston, and her parents may not have made a point of being there to say hello, but this place? This always felt like home.

Mac handled the traffic with ease, and they found a good spot to drop Joel and Chloe off. After that, she directed him to Stewart Beach, which was the place she always wanted to go as a child. That's where it seemed like all the families went, and watching the kids play with their dogs looked like so much fun.

Usually, her parents preferred East Beach because it was the only beach where alcohol was allowed.

They found a place to park. Sedona opened her door, breathed in the salty air, and stretched the muscles that were still tight from their long drive, not to mention the stress and tension of the last few weeks. She waited for Mac to grab a small backpack out of the van and lock it. Together they walked to the edge of the beach where she slipped off her shoes and socks.

Sedona's feet sank into the sand just enough that it took more effort to walk as they headed toward the water. The afternoon sun warmed her skin as the breeze carried in the smell of the ocean. It was a beautiful day. The only thing that might make it more perfect was if it were warm enough to let the waves crash over her feet.

They walked along the beach in companionable silence, just out of reach of the waves. She'd intentionally chosen the direction opposite East Beach. There were more people out than she thought there might be on a Sunday in the middle of December, but she supposed other people wanted to take advantage of the beautiful weather.

Between the roar of the waves, the seagulls calling overhead, and the murmur of people in the distance, it was the perfect combination to help her get out of her head.

"This seems to be your happy place."

"Yeah, I guess it is." She stopped and faced the ocean, where several ships dotted the horizon. "There's something about coming out here that always made all my problems seem so small in comparison. Like, if I stood here long enough, the waves would carry them away like they did everything else they touched." She shrugged. Maybe that sounded silly to him, but it was true.

"I totally get that. Sometimes, I think we have to remove ourselves from all the day-to-day noise and remind ourselves what's important."

She could feel him watching her for several moments before he took his backpack off one shoulder and unzipped the largest compartment.

"I borrowed a towel from the hotel. Do you want to sit for

a while?" He produced a perfectly-folded towel and shook it out before spreading it out on the dry sand.

Sedona chuckled as she claimed a spot on the towel. "Thank you. You came prepared."

"I try." He dropped his backpack on the sand, did a quick scan of the area around them, and then sat next to her.

She'd almost forgotten about the stalker. Obviously, he hadn't, which was exactly why she'd hired him to accompany them on the tour in the first place. "And you're always on the job."

To her surprise, he flinched at that. It was a tiny tightening of his mouth and the way his eyes narrowed slightly that clued her in. If she hadn't been watching him right then, she never would've known.

"I wouldn't be much use in private security if my clients were hurt under my watch." His response was matter-of-fact as he watched a piece of seaweed slowly get carried to shore wave after wave.

"I'm sorry. I didn't mean anything by that. If it helps, I'm actually impressed that you've stayed vigilant. I'm sure there are probably other things you'd rather be doing today, like relaxing at the hotel, instead of following me all over the place."

"Actually, there isn't." He glanced at her before turning his gaze forward again. "You have no reason to apologize. You said something that reminded me of a difficult conversation in the past. That's all."

Sedona was still trying to digest that first sentence. Did he truly mean it? That he'd rather be walking the beach with her than sleeping in or relaxing back at the hotel? She tried not to read into it, but knowing that he didn't resent being there with her did more for her self-confidence than it probably should have. Sometimes it bothered her that the fact her parents were always in a hurry to go off and leave her behind had made such a lasting impression on her. Mostly because she hated the idea that they still had that much power over her thoughts, even now.

She stretched her legs out, then settled back, her hands sinking into the towel behind her as she propped herself up. The breeze was still a bit chilly, but the sun overhead warmed her nicely, and she was considering ditching the coat.

Mac seemed to take his cue from her. He moved the backpack behind him so he could lean against it and crossed his legs in front of him. "I was married once. A long time ago—or at least it feels like it. Cassie and I met in college and got married as soon as we graduated. It didn't last quite two years."

He used to be married? The sudden jealousy toward someone she'd never met came out of nowhere. A jealousy she certainly had no right to feel.

"What happened?" The words were out before she could rein them in, and she instantly regretted it. "I'm sorry. It's none of my business. I can only imagine how difficult that must have been to go through. Especially since you were both so young."

They sat in silence long enough that she thought the conversation was over. Finally, he took a deep breath. "Cassie was not a fan of our family business, and she was even less thrilled when I took jobs that required any kind of travel. She was convinced I was trying to put space between us. Trying to get away from her." He shrugged as though it was no big deal, but it was clear Cassie's words had cut him to the core. "In an effort to fix things between us, I decided to take a step back and manage things from home base. But as soon as I told her that, she informed me that it was too little too late—that I was always on the job no matter what—and asked for a divorce."

The residual pain in his voice made her own heart hurt. Sure, she hadn't known him long. But if the esteem he'd earned from his family, the kindness she'd seen for herself, and his dedication to his job meant anything, it only increased her respect for him.

"It sounds like she was looking for an excuse to leave, and that's the one she chose to go with. If you'd walked away from private security completely, there may have been a different reason later. Obviously, I never met her, and I can't possibly know the situation, but maybe it had a lot more to do with her than it did with you."

He looked at her in surprise, and for the first time since she'd met him, he seemed at a loss for words. He reached for a smooth stone that was partially buried in the sand nearby. "Thank you for that. My mom told me the same at the time, but I wasn't ready to hear it then. It took a long while to let go of the guilt. I figured there had to be something I was doing wrong that caused her to be so unhappy."

Sedona sat up straight and reached over to rest her hand on the sleeve of his jacket. "Sometimes those scars run way deeper than they should, and they never heal completely."

Mac glanced at her hand, and she withdrew it, not wanting him to feel uncomfortable. She shrugged out of her coat and piled it on the ground beside her. The sun had finally warmed her up enough that the thick sweater she wore was enough. At least until the wind picked up again. These warmer December days were likely to fade soon.

"Sounds like you speak from experience. Is that why you're not married yet?"

He took off his own coat.

Sedona hesitated to respond to his question, but he'd shared a lot about himself, and it couldn't have been easy. It only seemed fair to return the favor.

She drew her knees to her chest and wrapped her arms around them. "I mentioned how my parents thought kids were better seen than heard. It seemed like every decision I made disappointed them." She focused on the waves and continued. "I grew up hearing my mother tell me that I needed to find a man who made enough money to take care of me so she and my dad didn't have to do that for the rest of my life. I mean, to my father's credit, he does do that for her, but he's not there for her emotionally or vice versa. Once I made it clear I was going to pursue a career in singing, and I signed with the label, Mom told me that no man was going to want to deal with my kind of drama. That anyone who was interested in me would only be there for the money. The day I walked away from the label, she had no problem letting me know that I'd thrown away any chance I had to find a man who would put up with my choices in life."

When she finally looked at Mac, she found him watching her with a mix of unbelief and anger on his face. "I can't even imagine discouraging someone like that, much less your only child. I hope you know none of that is true."

"I mean, technically, I know it's not. But I've heard it all my life, and the few men who were interested drifted away once they knew more about what I did. Mom says I pushed them away, and maybe that's true, even if I didn't mean to."

He leaned over to nudge her arm with his. "Like you said, some scars go way deeper than they look."

She nodded and nudged him back in a playful manner. Except this time, instead of them leaning away from each other, they simply sat in companionable silence. Sedona could feel his warmth seeping through the sleeve of her sweater, and it seemed like every sound—every breath—was accentuated.

She was trying to convince herself to enjoy the moment and not overthink it when Mac's cell phone pinged with a text.

"If I don't check it, that's a surefire way to guarantee it'll be important." He pulled it out of his jacket pocket and read the text. The expression on his face went from relaxed to all business. "Asher has news about Nick."

NINETEEN

Mac got to his feet and then reached down to help Sedona up. The moment her slender hand slid into his, he was tempted to continue holding it even after she'd regained her balance. Instead, he let go and retrieved his coat, the towel, and his backpack.

"He wants to talk to us through video, but I'm not sure how well we'll be able to hear with the waves. Why don't we go back to the van, see what Asher has, and then stop somewhere to get something to drink? After that, we can walk on the beach some more before it's time to meet the others for dinner."

He didn't want this time with her to end, but it was good Asher texted when he did. They'd both shared a lot more than they probably should have given their current arrangement.

Sedona tied her jacket around her waist and nodded. "That sounds like a good idea." The breeze on the beach had worked some of her hair loose from her ponytail, and it hung in sections by her ear.

He thought he caught a bit of disappointment in her voice, but then again, maybe he was just projecting his own.

Annoyed with himself for getting too personal, he led the way back to the van. Once they were settled inside, he started a video call to Asher.

"Hey, guys," his younger brother greeted them. "I know you wanted to hear as soon as we got anything else on Nick."

At the same time, Mac and Sedona leaned an elbow on the console between them so they could both see Asher and he could see them. Mac tried to ignore the way the smell of the ocean air mixed with honeysuckle to create an entirely memorable combination. "Absolutely. What did you find?"

"Officer Carrington was able to track down one of the women who had originally filed charges, gotten a restraining order, but eventually dropped all charges. Originally, she was reluctant to talk to him, and her identity wasn't shared with me. However, she finally decided to tell her story in case it would help.

"According to her, she and Nick were dating for several months when they had an argument over whether to attend a party. She didn't want to because she had a paper to write, and he insisted that she had to go with him because he wasn't going to go alone. When she refused, he told her that if she didn't go, they were through. Given the intensity of his reaction, she decided that ending their relationship would be best. Over the course of the following two weeks, he showed up everywhere, followed her, and even spoke to her friends to have them convince her to get back together with him. Eventually, he showed up at her dorm room and tried to kick down the door. She opened it, and he shoved her hard enough to send her to the floor. It was after that she filed for a restraining order."

Mac had a hard time reconciling this alleged side of Nick with what he'd seen so far. Yes, Nick got in Sedona's space more than he should've once, but that was a far cry from what he was hearing now.

If the perplexed expression on Sedona's face was any indication, she was surprised as well.

Asher got a drink and continued. "Once the restraining order was filed, he left her alone. Completely. Like, he even withdrew from the one class they both had and didn't speak to her again. That's why she eventually dropped the charges."

"That's so odd." Sedona rested her chin on the back of her left hand. "What about the other woman?"

"The story is very similar. They dated for a while, and everything was going well until he wanted her to move in with him, and she said it was too soon. He got angry, tried to force her to go with him to see the apartment he'd apparently already rented for them. She freaked out, tried to get out of his grasp, and he shoved her into the wall hard enough to break her wrist. According to her, he followed her to the ER, kept apologizing, and wouldn't leave her alone. She eventually filed her own restraining order. Like before, as soon as she did, he disappeared from her life. It made more sense to drop the charges and move on."

"I almost wonder if he'd had problems with substance abuse at that point in his life. It might explain why he was so different in those two instances from the way he seems today." Mac frowned. Maybe, after the second incident, Nick realized he needed to do something to fix his problem, and he got help? Mac would feel a lot better about that if Nick were happily married now rather than still single.

"Even if that was true, it's a big part of his personality that he's kept hidden, and he's never said anything directly to me about being interested in me or wanting me to go out with him." Sedona used both hands to sweep some of the loose sections of her hair behind her ears. "I'm racking my brain here, and I truly can't figure out what I might have done to trigger him." There was a barely perceptible catch in her voice.

"Hey." Mac waited for her to turn her head and look at

him. "Even if it *is* Nick, and he's obsessed with you, it's not your fault. You've done nothing to deserve this." He held her gaze until she finally nodded her acknowledgment.

Asher was watching them, and Mac noticed a curiosity in his brother's eyes that he chose to ignore. "I wish we knew what Nick was doing now."

"Me, too," Sedona muttered.

"I'm sorry, guys. I wish I had more." Asher folded his hands in front of his chin. "Keep an eye on Nick, and I think Officer Carrington is still digging. Let us know if you find out anything at all. In the meantime, I hope today has been a good break so far. You've earned it."

"It has, Asher. Thanks for letting us know. Tell everyone I said hi."

"Will do."

The video call ended, and Mac turned off the phone. "Well, I'm really not sure what we're supposed to do with *that* information."

"And we have to keep acting like we did before we knew all this, because Nick doesn't know that we know." A little smile tugged at the corners of her mouth. "You know?"

He chuckled. "Yes, I know." That she was able to find some humor in the moment made him like her even more. "Come on, I saw a coffee shop earlier. Let's see if they serve tea, too."

Twenty minutes later, they each had a paper cup in hand. He thought Sedona would want to order tea since they did have several varieties on the menu, but when they saw that peppermint hot chocolate was available, they both decided on it.

They took their time enjoying their drinks as they meandered their way back toward the beach. Sedona seemed to be lost in thought, and so they walked in near silence until the sand met the waves, and then they turned to walk along the shoreline.

By then, they'd both finished their drinks. Mac stacked their cups and put them in the side pocket of his backpack to throw away later.

"Should I cancel the tour?"

Her question was so out of left field that Mac stopped walking. "What?"

She turned to face him and squared her shoulders as though this was something she'd been gathering the courage to ask for a while, and maybe she had. "With everything going on, maybe it'd be better if I canceled the tour and sent everyone home. I mean, after what happened with the tires, it's clear I'm not the only one who might be in danger. If any of the others got hurt, I'd never forgive myself."

Her words came faster as she spoke, as though she were trying to get everything she was thinking out in the open before she lost her nerve.

Sedona held her hands up in frustration. "It would help if I knew what this guy wanted. I mean, is this specifically about my music or this tour? Is he punishing me for something he thinks I did? Or is it all about control? Making me fear the next time he strikes? If we don't figure out who he is, and he keeps coming after me, then if I keep the tour going, I'm just putting everyone else at risk."

Angry tears filled her eyes, and Mac desperately wanted to find the man who was causing her this anguish.

"Come here." He reached for her, and she immediately stepped into his arms. He cautioned himself to keep the hug friendly, much like he might hug and comfort Erica if she'd needed it.

But the moment her arms went around his waist and squeezed tight, all those thoughts evaporated. Sedona's trust in him caused something to shift in his heart, and he knew that no matter what happened with the case or how things stood between them when it was all over, it would be difficult to walk away from her.

Mac reached up and cradled the back of her neck with one palm. The hair from her ponytail brushed against the back of his hand as her sweet scent surrounded him. Never mind the ocean waves or the peace of the beach. This, right here, was his new happy place, and that created a new problem—one he wasn't ready to address yet.

TWENTY

Between the sun warming the top of her head, the soothing rhythm of the waves, and the strong arms holding her close, Sedona would've been happy to stay right there forever. At least, right now, the threat of her stalker seemed miles away.

"We're going to figure this out." Mac's voice, which sounded slightly husky, caused deep vibrations in his chest.

She focused on his steady heartbeat. She wanted to believe his words, but right now, she had no idea how to do that.

He must've sensed her hesitation because he gently grasped her upper arms and took a step back so he could see her face. "I mean it, Sedona. We're not going to rest until we know who's responsible and make sure they never bother you again."

The intensity in his gaze told her he was serious, and he believed every word. The problem was, what happened once the tour was over? If they hadn't caught the stalker by then, Mac would go back to Destiny because she couldn't afford to pay him indefinitely.

His attention shifted to her right cheek. With a single

fingertip, he collected a lock of her hair and tucked it behind her ear, his touch igniting a flurry of sensations across her cheek and releasing a whole swarm of butterflies in her stomach.

When his gaze locked with hers, she thought he might lean in and kiss her. Instead, he blinked and took another step back before gripping the straps of his backpack with his hands.

"Come on, let's find a spot to sit again. Then we'll go over everything and come up with a plan. Okay?"

Sedona wasn't sure what kind of plan they'd be able to construct when they didn't know who was after her in the first place, but it sounded good. It was a whole lot better than not being proactive about it in general.

"Yeah. Okay."

Mac got the towel back out and spread it on the sand. Instead of looking out over the water, he turned and faced her. "The first thing I want to make very clear is that I don't plan to walk away until we've figured this out. I'm hoping and praying that it'll be before the end of your tour. But if it's not, I'm going to keep you safe for as long as it takes."

She dreaded the day he went back to his life, and hers continued in the opposite direction. However, knowing that he'd be there to watch her back until then brought a great deal of peace. She'd figure out how to pay him when that time came.

For now, none of her money meant a thing if something happened to her.

"That means a lot. Thank you."

They were both sitting cross-legged on the towel, and their knees were a breath away from brushing against each other.

Sedona scooped up a little sand in one hand and slowly spread her fingers and let it fall, grain by grain, into her other palm. A few bounced off and landed on her pants near her knee. She tossed the rest back onto the beach where it belonged. "I meant what I said about canceling the rest of the tour. I think it's something to consider for the good of everyone involved."

Mac watched her thoughtfully for several moments, then looked out at the waves as they lapped at the shore.

"My instinct is to keep everything going just like it is. Like you said, this guy hasn't told you anything about what he does or doesn't want from you. Maybe ending the tour means he'll move on, and that'll be the end of it. Or it could put him into hiding for a while, only to have him re-emerge next time you're on tour. I'm also worried that, if he does have a goal or purpose, and you cancel the tour, he's going to have to speed up his time frame, which could be even more dangerous."

"None of these scenarios is making me feel any better."

"I know, and I'm sorry." He reached out and brushed the sand from her knee. "The thing is, I'd rather smoke him out now. He's been active, and he's eventually going to make a mistake. We'll be right there waiting for him when he does. That said, you're right. It's not fair to the others to be put in a dangerous position without giving them the option to bow out if they want to. I think you should talk to them tonight and see what they say."

She nodded. "I'm glad you feel that way, too. Whether they want to stay or go, at least they can make a more informed decision. We'll deal with whatever needs to be done once we know." She'd bet on Chloe and Lou staying. She had no idea about the others.

Then there was Nick. If he was the one behind the threats, would he insist on staying so he could keep an eye on things? Or would he be happy stepping away, giving him more time to continue his harassment?

The unknowns were about to drive her insane.

The only constant right now was Mac's promise to stay by her side no matter which direction things took.

"The fact is, you've only got about a week left in your tour. This guy enjoys the attention. I have a feeling he's going to make a move—and soon."

"What makes you say that?"

"Because, despite everything he's done, you've had the courage to keep pressing forward. I doubt he accounted for that when he targeted you, and it's likely starting to irritate him."

There was a hint of humor in his expression, and under the open sky with the ocean nearby, his eyes took on a blue shade instead of their usual hazel. "You are a force to be reckoned with, Sedona Reeves."

His compliment, along with the warmth in his expression, sent her heart racing. "Thank you." She ducked her chin and turned her attention back to the waves.

They chatted about random things until, half an hour later, the wind started to pick up. It kept whipping the corners of the towel over, and because of how they were sitting, Sedona's ponytail continuously blew into her face.

The wind was cool, and she shivered. They only had an hour until dinner with Chloe and Joel, which meant their time at the beach was coming to an end. Even still, she didn't look forward to leaving it behind.

"We should probably head back," Mac said, although he sounded about as reluctant as she did.

"Yeah. I suppose so."

Disappointment hit hard, but he was right. By the time they walked back to the car and then drove to the restaurant, it'd be about time. And after sitting out there in the wind, Sedona could only imagine how messy her hair looked. She reached up and released it from the elastic band before shaking it out a little.

A hand appeared in front of her, and Mac helped her to her feet, then picked up her jacket and handed it to her.

She tied it around her waist, figuring the walk back to the van would warm her up again.

They both stepped off the towel and onto the beach. The wind snagged it, and Mac had to move quickly to snatch it before it blew away. "I have a feeling the hotel keeps track of these. I really don't want them to charge you extra."

"Well, if it happened, it would've been worth it." She watched as he rolled the towel up and shoved it into his backpack before shouldering it. "Thanks for being willing to escort me today. I wanted to come here for the ocean, but the company made the experience even better."

Did she really just say that? It was certainly true, but now it sounded like she was flirting with him. Was she? Her cheeks turned pink and, embarrassed, she turned to walk back in the direction they had come from earlier.

"Sedona." Mac snagged her hand and gently tugged her back around to face him. "I thoroughly enjoyed getting to spend the afternoon with you." He lightly ran his thumb over the top of her hand. "If our situations were different..."

"I know." She tried to suppress her disappointment and gave him a smile she hoped passed as normal. He was right, they were on two very different paths, but out here it would be far too easy to pretend none of that mattered. She withdrew her hand from his and pointed out a ship on the horizon as they began to walk.

At least, in a different scenario, it was nice to know he might've been interested in her. That would have to be enough.

At dinner, it was hard not to say anything to Chloe and Joel about whether they should cancel the tour, but Sedona wanted the chance to talk to everyone at once. Besides, it would give Mac the opportunity to observe all their immediate reactions. The only one who wouldn't be there was

Connor, but that didn't matter since he was only accompanying them because her parents were paying him to.

Sedona copied Chloe and enjoyed a big bowl of clam chowder for dinner. It was so good that, even though she was stuffed, it left her wishing she had room for more.

The drive back to the hotel was a quiet one. Mac put on some music for background noise. Joel napped part of the way, and at least once, Sedona found herself drifting off to sleep.

Once back at the hotel, Sedona groaned as she climbed out of the van. All that walking followed by sitting for a while had made her leg muscles stiff.

"Hey, Chloe? Joel? I know we all want to change and crash, but I really wanted to talk to everyone. Could you drop by my room in about an hour?"

"You got it." Joel gave her a salute and headed for his room. If he was worried or all that curious, he sure didn't show it.

Chloe, however, furrowed her brow, worry etched on her face. "Is everything okay?" She glanced at Mac and then back again.

"I just want to get everyone's opinion on something and figured it'd be easier to bring it up one time." Sedona gave her friend a hug. "I'm glad you had fun shopping. The trip was great."

"Yeah, it was. I'm glad we made sure to schedule in the day off." Chloe smiled, although her eyes still shone with concern. "I'll see you in an hour."

That left Mac and Sedona in the hallway just down from their rooms. He motioned toward her door. "Shall we?"

"We shall." She used her key card to unlock the door.

Mac went in before her and checked the room first. "Yours is clear, and we left the connecting door open. I'll go check mine and let you get some downtime. Are you going to text the others about the meeting?"

"Yes, I was just about to—"

Someone knocked loudly on her door.

Mac quickly crossed the room and looked through the peephole. "It's Lou."

He stepped back, giving her room to open the door.

"Lou? Is everything okay?"

He looked from Sedona to Mac and then back again. "Not exactly. We've got a problem."

TWENTY-ONE

The whole group sat in Sedona's hotel room and watched the local news on the television. Smoke poured from the community center where they were supposed to perform tomorrow night. While they couldn't see the flames, it was nearly dark, and the windows of the building were lit with an eerie yellow-orange glow.

Mac sat perched on the arm of the couch, hating the feeling of defeat that filled the room.

"At least no one was hurt." Chloe shook her head, her eyes teary.

"Even if they can get that fire out before it takes the whole building, it'll take a while to rebuild or repair the damage," Nick agreed.

Sedona didn't say anything from her spot on the edge of the bed, but when she met Mac's eyes, he knew exactly what she was thinking. She was worried that the stalker was responsible for setting the fire. It certainly crossed Mac's mind. The fact was, there was no way to know. Certainly not yet. Chances were, the fire department didn't even know how the fire had originated yet.

"It's a huge hit for that community." Lou kept his eyes on

the television as he shook his head sadly. "The center gave at-risk kids a place to go to after school, not to mention the huge senior program they had going. We didn't get paid nearly as much for playing there as we might have in other places, but I figured it was worth it. Saw it as more of an outreach than anything."

Mac got the sense that Lou may have benefited from the same type of center when he was a kid.

After getting to her feet, Sedona paced to the door of the hotel room and back again. "Look, I wanted to talk to you all tonight anyway. When we started out on this tour, none of you signed up for slashed tires, threats, loose lug nuts, and fires." She waved at the television. "I don't want any of you to feel obligated to stay for the rest of this tour. If we need to cancel, then so be it."

Chloe, who had been lounging on the bed, sat up straight and stared at Sedona as though her friend had grown antlers. "You mean, let the stalker win?"

"That's part of the problem. We don't know what the stalker's goal is, other than to try to scare me. I don't want to risk anyone getting hurt. If you'd rather go home and put this behind you, I promise I will not hold it against you." Sedona jammed her hands into the pockets of her jeans and looked right at Joel. "What do you want to do?"

He looked from her to Chloe and back. "I was the kid who, when the bully picked on me in middle school, just made sure to punch him harder. Solved the problem. I have no intention of walking away."

"How about you, Nick?"

Mac watched the other man carefully as he considered his answer. "It feels a lot like we've been trying to swim against the current on this tour. That said, I don't particularly appreciate someone else trying to dictate what we can and can't do. I vote we keep going."

"Same." Lou held up a hand and then pointed at the TV.

"This may or may not be related, but if this stalker thinks we're gonna tuck tail and run, he's dead wrong."

A small smile pulled at Sedona's lips. She turned to her friend. "Chloe?"

"I'd be lying if I said all of this wasn't scary. But I'm with the others. I say we stick it out and finish this tour strong." She shifted to sit cross-legged. "Ultimately, though, I want to support you. What do *you* want to do? Because you're the one in the crosshairs. If you think we need to call it and get back home, then that's one hundred percent what's going to happen."

Sedona's shoulders squared, and she lifted her chin. "I'm not going to let someone scare us away from doing something we were called to do. If you guys are willing, then I say we keep pushing forward."

Plenty of people would've backed down and gone home. It certainly would've been the easier option. But not Sedona. She truly was one of the strongest people Mac had ever known.

"Now that we've got that out of the way," Joel stood, "I may have an idea. What if we hold the concert tomorrow anyway and ask for donations to benefit the rebuilding of the community center?"

"Oh, I love that!" Chloe clasped her hands together. "I just hope we can find somewhere indoors to perform."

Everyone in the room laughed.

Sedona reached for a pad of paper and pen that the hotel left on the table. "Hopefully, a concert at the same time, even if the location has to change, will encourage everyone who bought tickets to come and not ask for refunds." She wrote something down. "Now, I know this concert, like the others, is supposed to bring in some revenue for us, but what if we donated all *our* proceeds to the community center? I'm only suggesting it. No one should be forced to go that route."

"I'm good with that," Joel immediately said with conviction, and the others quickly agreed.

Sedona's chin quivered, and her eyes filled with tears. "That's what this is ultimately about, right? To share our music with others and encourage them? What better way to do that than to help a community facing a loss like this right before Christmas?"

Mac had a great deal of respect for her before and genuinely liked her. Now, it was clear she was as beautiful on the inside as she was on the outside.

He should've been proud of himself for making it through the whole day with her and managing to keep their relationship at a working friendship level. After all, he'd been tempted to kiss her on more than one occasion.

If he were honest with himself, though, he truly regretted not pulling her close and showing her how, after not even a week, she'd completely gotten under his skin. If he'd done that at the beginning of their trip to the beach, how different might their day have been?

Sedona's voice brought Mac's attention back to the room. "Nick, will you please hook the trailer back up to the van first thing in the morning? That way, if we need to change locations on the spur of the moment tomorrow, we'll be ready. Lou? Do you have any way to get in contact with someone from the community center?"

"I don't know if I'll be able to get a hold of anyone tonight, but I can at least leave some messages." Lou rubbed his hands together. "I'm going back to my room. All the venue information is in there, and I'll start researching alternative locations." With that, he waved and left.

Everyone else in the room started talking about possibilities, how they might change their setup if they did have to play outdoors, and a few other scenarios.

Mac liked the whole idea of the benefit concert. It was an amazing way to not only help the community that was going to be negatively affected by the fire, but to show the stalker and potential arsonist that this wasn't going to stop them. However, the unknown venue and potentially much larger crowd were going to result in a situation that would be a nightmare to control. Especially now that, more than ever, Sedona's life may be in jeopardy.

The others were still talking excitedly as he walked through the open doors to his room. He'd barely taken his phone out of his pocket when footsteps brought his attention around to Sedona standing in the doorway.

"Is everything okay?"

"Yeah." He lifted his phone. "I was just going to call Asher and let him know what was happening. With any luck, Officer Carrington in Destiny might be able to reach out to whoever is investigating the community center fire. I'm hoping we can find out whether arson is suspected, even if that detail hasn't been made public yet."

She crossed her arms and took several steps forward. "I probably should've gotten your take on the benefit concert before we moved forward with the plan. I apologize for that."

"You don't need to apologize. I think you guys are doing the right thing. I'm not going to lie, this could be a logistical nightmare from a private security perspective, but we're going to get it figured out."

"And if the stalker really is responsible for this fire?"

"Then he's going to have one more set of charges to face when we finally catch him."

TWENTY-TWO

S edona got out of the van to take in their surroundings, and her heart filled to the brim. In less than twenty-four hours, the community had pulled together what she would always remember as a miracle. Not only was the idea of holding a benefit concert embraced with open arms, but it had been amazing to watch everyone come together to make it possible.

A makeshift stage had been constructed in the parking lot in front of the damaged community center. While the temperature was going to drop overnight, right now it was in the low sixties with next to no wind. That felt like a miracle all on its own.

Several food trucks were set up and had promised to donate a part of their proceeds to the cause as well, and picnic tables had been brought in to give people a place to sit and eat.

What began as a concert had already turned into so much more, and the evening hadn't even started yet.

Lou already had the soundboard set up, and they were ready to go. It was just a matter of waiting until it was time to take the stage.

The energy of the people milling around made Sedona both excited and nervous.

"This has turned into quite the crowd," Connor commented. He'd arrived at the hotel half an hour before they all got in the van and headed over.

Sedona didn't miss the way he exchanged a concerned look with Mac, which only made her nerves worse.

The large turnout was a true gift because it likely meant the community center would receive significant support through donations.

With so many people present, Connor and Mac's ability to oversee the situation was severely limited. Keeping track of everything would be next to impossible.

"It sure has," she murmured. She needed something to take her mind off the fact that her stalker could be out there somewhere right now. "I'm glad you and your wife got to spend some time together. Less than a week, and you'll be back home again. I'm sure you're both ready."

"It will be nice." Connor smiled. "Jill is planning to come down tonight to listen. I'll try to introduce you after the concert if that's okay."

"I'd like that."

Lou appeared and helped Sedona get her IEM set up. She slipped the earpiece in and immediately took it back out again. He noticed and gave her a quizzical look.

"I'm going to wait until we're a little closer to showtime." Memories of the creepy voice coming through her headphones last time made her shiver. The stalker had no problem accessing it back in Austin, and there were way more people here tonight for him to blend in with.

Lou gave her shoulder a supportive squeeze.

Mac, who hadn't been far away all day, appeared at her side. "Remember, stay away from the edges of the stage."

She chuckled. "Someone steals my shoe *one time,* and you never let me forget it. I promise I won't crowd surf."

That earned her a hearty laugh.

"I'm relieved to hear that." He looked at her in amusement. "I'm going to be on your right near the stage, and Connor will be taking a position on your left. You'll be able to see both of us the entire time." His phone pinged, and he took it out of his pocket. "It's a text from Asher. The local fire and police departments have no reason to believe the fire was arson. More investigation is needed, but they think it was caused by a short in the utility room."

So the stalker wasn't behind the fire after all? Could it really have been a terrible accident and a coincidence? That realization lifted the heavy burden of guilt she'd been carrying, making her aware of just how much she'd blamed herself for bringing the stalker here.

That didn't mean he wasn't out there somewhere, though. She fingered the earbud that she really did need to put in her ear.

Mac noticed. Seriously, did anything get by him? "There's only so much you can control. Focus on that and keep your chin up. Can I pray for you?"

Her eyes widened, and she found herself nodding.

He placed a hand on each shoulder and bowed his head. "Father God, we thank You for the grace You've shown this community and for our small part in making a difference. I pray for Your protection over Sedona and the rest of the group. Give Sedona the strength and courage she needs tonight. May You bless those who hear her music. Amen."

"Amen." The pressure on her chest eased a little.

"You've got this."

Joel jogged up. "They're ready for us."

Sedona flashed Mac a grin. "No. *We've* got this." With that, she put her earbud in and followed Joel to where the others were waiting for them.

The crowd cheered as they took the stage.

Sedona waved. "Hello, Houston!" More cheers erupted.

"It's truly an honor to be here tonight. The way you all have come together is a true testament to the strength of your community. This, right here, is what's important. This isn't just an example of the holiday spirit or neighbors helping neighbors. What we're seeing here is the love of God at work."

She scanned the crowd that cheered even louder, and her gaze snagged on Mac. He was watching her, and his expression softened. He gave her an approving nod.

"All right, what do you say we get this concert started?"

They'd returned to the hotel an hour ago, and Sedona still couldn't shake off the buzz of excitement. The crowd seemed to love the music, and a local news station had even interviewed them all about their role in bringing the benefit concert to life. After their show, they'd stuck around to encourage the next group and got something to eat from the food trucks before leaving. Mac and Connor weighed the risks, and everyone had agreed that it was worth staying to support the cause.

Having Jill there made the evening even more enjoyable. The way Connor cared for his wife made it nearly unthinkable for Sedona to view him as a potential suspect anymore.

Considering how difficult the last two years had been—and even more the last five weeks—the successful concert and amazing night were exactly what she needed to keep moving forward.

They could make a difference. Her *music* could make a difference.

Now, Sedona was exhausted, but there was no way she was going to be able to sleep yet, especially after such an amazing day. She showered, changed into her comfortable lounge pants and cozy shirt, and then sat down at the little table to work on a new song she'd been inspired by the other day.

She looked longingly at the guitar case on the other side of the room.

That was one bad thing about staying in hotels—it was late enough that she didn't dare pick up her guitar and start playing. At home, that would've been the first thing she'd do.

Instead, she worked on the lyrics as she hummed the tune that was already taking shape in her heart.

After that, she pulled her Bible and devotional book out and spent some time with them.

It was nearly one in the morning before she finally felt tired enough to go to bed. Once she did, sleep came almost instantly.

Partway through the night, she started to dream. Even as she walked into the ground floor of a giant skyscraper, Sedona somehow knew it wasn't real, yet she couldn't make herself wake up. She was compelled to get into the elevator. She started out alone as she pushed the button for the very top floor. One by one, as they passed each floor, more people got onto the elevator until she was pressed against the wall in the very back.

Sedona never had issues with claustrophobia. Right now, though, it felt as though she had to force each breath as she fought against the panic.

As they neared the top of the skyscraper, people started to exit the elevator one or two at a time until she had room to move. She breathed in deeply as relief poured over her like water.

Finally, only she and another passenger remained as they reached the top floor. The man in front of her kept his back to her.

The elevator came to an abrupt stop.

Ping!

The doors slid open, and the man in front of her took a

large step forward, placing his shoe in front of the doors to keep them from closing, but he didn't exit the elevator.

The doors tried to shut and, once they sensed something was in the way, they opened again.

Ping!

Sedona couldn't remember why she needed to get to that top floor. All she knew was that she needed to get out of the elevator. Now. Or she was going to be late.

"Excuse me, sir. Could I step past you?"

He didn't move. Not even a slight shift in position

Ping!

She started to step around him. That's when he faced her. He didn't turn. One second, his back was to her, and the next, he was staring at her like something out of a horror movie.

Black ski mask but with a space for the mouth. Dark eyes that didn't look human. And a grin.

Ping!

Sedona jumped away from him, her arm striking something to her side.

The next thing she knew, she was in her hotel room, sitting upright in her bed. She must've flailed her arms because everything on the side table had been knocked onto the floor, including a cup of water.

The fear from her dream, coupled with the strange environment, and her breath came quickly as her heart pounded in her chest.

She threw the covers aside, pushed the button to turn on the light above the bed, and scrambled to make sure the water from the cup hadn't doused her phone or the hotel alarm clock.

The carpet absorbed most of the water. Feeling numb, she sank to her knees, blindly reached her hand under the bed, and swept back and forth until her fingers connected with the phone. She dragged the screen across her shirt to wipe off the moisture. That's when she noticed she'd received four texts.

The pings from the elevator in her dreams.

Distracted, she lifted the alarm clock to set it back on the side table. She wasn't paying enough attention, and when she moved her arm away, it caught on the electrical cord and jerked it back off the table with an even louder clatter.

Groaning, she finally put it back in its place, tossed the paper cup in the trash, and got to her feet.

Only then did she allow herself to focus on the texts again. She'd just swiped to read them when a gentle knock came from the connecting doors. "Sedona? Are you okay?"

His voice faded to the background as the texts popped up. All from the same unknown caller. She froze in place.

You've got everyone else fooled.

But I know the real you.

You only think you're safe.

One day you'll know the truth.

TWENTY-THREE

When a noise woke Mac up originally, he didn't think much of it. Hotels in general were relatively loud places with people coming and going at all hours of the night. Still, he'd sat up in bed and listened. This time, when a muffled crash came from Sedona's room, he jumped up and pulled on his jeans. Grabbing his holstered gun from the nightstand, he strode over to the connecting doors.

They'd continued to leave them unlocked even though they did keep them closed. Hesitant to just walk in unannounced, he opened his door and then knocked loudly enough on hers for her to hear it, but hopefully soft enough not to wake her up if he'd been mistaken and she was still fast asleep.

"Sedona? Are you okay?"

No response, and he didn't hear anything else coming from her room.

"Sedona?"

Before he had to make a decision, the knob turned, and the door opened, ushering in a gentle hint of honeysuckle.

Sedona stood in front of him in a pair of lounge pants, an

oversized sweatshirt, and bare feet. Her hair was tousled. "I had a nightmare and knocked everything off the side table." She motioned to the bed behind her. "Then I saw these."

She held her phone out.

He took it and read through the texts that were sent in succession. The worry that'd built up earlier was quickly replaced with anger.

"Apparently, I'm loud when I get startled. Funny the things we don't know about ourselves until we're being stalked." Her voice held layers of sarcasm. There was no humor on her face, though, and the shadows beneath her eyes spoke of her exhaustion.

What she needed was a break from all of this. He prayed they'd find out who was behind the threats before the situation escalated further. Before it pushed her past her limits.

He put an arm around her shoulders and walked with her to the small table in his room. "Why don't you sit down for a few minutes? I'll take a picture of these and e-mail it to Asher. He won't be able to do anything until morning when he can reach out to Logan at DPD, but at least he'll have it when he wakes up."

Sedona nodded and took a seat. He set his gun back down on the side table and then sent the info to Asher.

He grabbed one of his favorite shirts and pulled it on over the T-shirt he'd worn to bed.

"When the tour is finished, I'm getting a new phone with a new number," she announced. "One that I'll only tell a handful of people. I mean, how did this guy even get this one in the first place?"

"Things like that aren't hard to find if you have the right resources."

"Like a brother in tech or connections to the local police department?" She raised a brow. "I'm kidding, by the way." A small smile lifted the corners of her mouth and brought a tiny sparkle to her eyes.

He chuckled. "I was thinking more like the willingness to dig in someone else's trash to find a phone bill or, really, any paperwork where you might have your phone number listed."

"Which is a lot, when you think about it. That's really creepy."

She wasn't wrong. Phone numbers were used everywhere from doctors' offices, the dry cleaners, and even the reward system set up with the grocery store.

"Yeah, it is. It's difficult to stay completely private in this day and age."

"In some ways, it was easier back when I had content that had just started to go viral. I got my music out there without having to deal with the in-person challenges. Sometimes I wish I could go back to that." She used her fingers to comb through her hair. "And then there are concerts like last night where so much would be lost if it weren't in person."

"Seeing everyone come together like that was one of the most inspirational things I've been a part of." He sat in the chair across from her. "I'm glad I was here to experience it. For what it's worth, it would be a real shame if you ever stepped away from the music industry. You've got a gift, Sedona. It's not just your music but the way you communicate and encourage others. You are truly the ray of sunshine that people need in their lives."

She'd certainly brightened his life with her bravery and tenacity.

"Thank you." She dipped her chin.

"I'm sorry about the nightmares. Was it related to the stalker?"

Sedona nodded. "Yeah, but it pulled in the sound of the texts coming to my phone. It was very disorienting."

She told him about the elevator ride and the pings. He knew it was just a dream, but thinking about the man in black blocking her exit still made him wish he could've been there to rescue her.

"You should try to get some more sleep. You've got to be exhausted after everything."

"Not going to happen. Not yet." She tilted her head toward the connecting doors. "I'm going to go make myself a cup of hot chocolate, try to get my mind off the dream and texts. Then I'll try."

"Chocolate does make everything better."

"Almost always." Sedona studied him for a moment. "I have enough if you care to join me."

"I'd like that. Thank you." He wasn't going to be able to go to sleep for a while either. He was worried about her, and he'd be wondering if she was okay if she'd just gone back to her room.

"I'll go turn the coffee pot on for some hot water." She stood and padded out of the room.

Mac wasn't surprised when he got a text from Asher.

> Just got your e-mail. I'll reach out to Logan first thing in the morning. Is Sedona okay?

His youngest brother didn't always keep traditional hours. Sometimes that was thanks to cases like this. Other times, it was simply because he tended to work better at night. Tonight, though, was his monthly Dungeons & Dragons game. Asher and his friends had been holding the game for nearly two years. Most of the time, it was on a Friday or Saturday night. With the holidays approaching, this was the only night that worked for everyone in December.

> She's shaken but doing okay. How's the game?

Great. Wrapping things up now. Gotta run, but message if anything else comes up. I'll reach out when I get news.

Will do. Good night.

Night.

Mac slipped his phone into his pocket and knocked on the connected doors. They were still open, but he didn't want to surprise her.

"Come on in." Her voice, no doubt quiet to keep from disturbing Chloe sleeping on the other side, came from around the corner where she was pouring hot water into two paper cups the hotel had provided. "Swiss Miss. It might not be fancy, but it does the job."

She emptied a packet into each cup. She must've gotten cold because her feet were now covered in thick, gray socks.

"Thank you." He accepted a cup along with a coffee stirrer and began to mix his hot chocolate. "There's not a thing wrong with Swiss Miss."

They stood in silence as they each sipped their drink. Simultaneously, they nodded in satisfaction, which brought muffled laughter as they tried to keep the noise down.

Mac motioned to the table that was strewn with papers. He'd noticed the Bible there as well. "Looks like you've been busy."

"I'm working on a song. My goal is to start recording a new album toward the end of January."

"Do you write all your own music?"

"Most of it. I've done a couple of collaborations, which were a lot of fun."

It amazed him that she not only knew how to play her guitar and sing so beautifully, but that she was able to write her own songs as well.

Seriously, Gilbert Remming with Moonlight Studios must have kicked himself every day for pushing his agenda and letting her go.

It wasn't going to be easy when this job was finished. Mac would have to walk away knowing he likely wouldn't see Sedona again outside of going to one of her concerts.

If things were different…

How many times had he thought that over the last few days?

He realized Sedona was watching him, a thoughtful expression on her face as she cupped her hot chocolate with both hands.

"So why do you do this? Work in private security? I mean, I know you said it's a family business, and it's clear everyone I've met so far takes the job very seriously. But you seem to have a true passion for helping others. Is there a particular reason?"

"The easy answer is that I grew up watching my dad do this and seeing the difference it made in people's lives."

"And the complicated one?"

He shrugged, then took one of the chairs when she motioned that he should sit. He waited for her to join him before he continued. "Part of it was Cole. I mean, if it weren't for my parents, he wouldn't have had anyone in his corner. They fought for him and provided that safe place. Cole will be the first to tell you that it saved his life. I guess that's why I do this. I want to be able to step in, fight for someone who needs help, and provide that safe place when they might not know where else to turn."

A little embarrassed for having said so much, he shrugged again and downed the rest of his hot chocolate.

Sedona's gaze was filled with both a deep respect and a wistfulness that made him desperately want to know what she was thinking.

It took everything in him not to reach across the table and

take her smaller hand in his. He pushed to his feet and walked over to the trash can near the bathroom to throw away his cup. "I should go and let you get some rest."

"Of course. I'm sure you're ready to get some sleep yourself." She stood and set her near-empty cup on the table. "I'm sorry I disturbed you tonight."

"You never have to apologize for that." Mac approached the table. "I'm here to watch your back, and that includes helping you deal with texts and nightmares caused by stalkers." He gave her an encouraging smile, hoping it would put her at ease. He meant every word of it.

Relief flashed in her eyes as her pretty smile returned. There was something about the way those creases at the corners of her mouth made her face radiate joy. He could get used to being the one who brought those smiles to life.

He moved toward the connecting door, and Sedona followed. "I'll be praying the rest of your night is a peaceful one. You should consider turning your phone to Do Not Disturb and trying to sleep in. Even if you miss the continental breakfast downstairs, I'm sure we can find someplace to get something for you to eat. It'd do you some good to catch up a little. Just text me once you're up and going for the day."

"Yeah. Maybe I will."

At least she was considering it. "Good night, Sedona."

He'd crossed over to his room when she spoke again behind him.

"Hey, Mac?"

"Yeah?" He turned around to face her.

"For the record, what you do makes a huge difference. It has in my situation." She drew in a breath, her posture softening as she hesitated. "This has all been such a nightmare, but it's you who's been that safe place for me."

Her words and vulnerability reached deep inside his heart and applied a thin layer of comfort over the wound that

Cassie had left after their divorce. Protecting Sedona was his job, but knowing that she felt safe with him... comfortable enough to share the things that matter to her...

He ought to go back to his room right now before he did something that would change everything. Yet, there she was, watching him with those eyes that he couldn't look away from.

Three steps were all it took for him to stand directly in front of her. He stopped short of reaching out to touch her, even though every cell in his body tried to convince him to do exactly that.

TWENTY-FOUR

Sedona's pulse thrummed in her ears. Mac stood before her, his imposing stature making her feel small, yet safe. Slowly, she brought her gaze from his shirt up to his face. It was the look in his eyes, the determination that gave way to a tenderness, that had made her heart tumble in her chest.

"Sunshine, this is a horrible idea," he said softly, his voice low and husky.

"I know."

He leaned in then, brushing his lips against hers in a whisper of a kiss that lasted only a few moments. When she opened her eyes, he was gazing at her, clearly looking for the answer to an unspoken question.

Sedona placed her hand against his chest. His heartbeat raced against her palm as he put an arm around her waist and pulled her close. This time, the fervor of his kiss stole her breath.

Everything she'd been worried about—everything that'd happened over the course of the tour—faded into the background until there was nothing but the mind-blowing intensity of being in his arms.

He turned them until her back was against the doorframe. She threaded her fingers into the hair at the base of his neck.

He kissed her again, letting his lips move from her mouth to the edge of her jaw. With a groan, he let his forehead rest against hers. "I really need to stop kissing you now, and you should get some rest."

"Yeah." Even with that single word, she sounded breathless, and Mac noticed. He gave her one more slow kiss before stepping away. He reached out to touch her chin with his thumb, then walked through the door, closing it softly behind him.

She released a lungful of air as she pushed hers closed.

In the bathroom, she looked at her reflection in the mirror. She cringed when she realized how messy her hair looked and sighed. She should've brushed it or something.

Obviously, Mac didn't mind. She touched a finger to her lips and smiled.

Those kisses had been more amazing than anything she could've imagined. She leaned against the counter and welcomed the feel of the cool surface against her heated skin.

Everything just got a whole lot more complicated. What if he realized kissing her was a mistake, and they still had to interact and spend time together?

What if it wasn't weird between them, and after this weekend, going their separate ways was like torture?

Nothing about the situation was going to be easy.

But try as she might, she couldn't regret kissing Mac.

She turned off the lights and climbed back into bed. She spent time praying for wisdom, guidance, and safety for everyone involved, especially Mac. She finally fell asleep thinking about the way it felt to be held in his arms.

Sedona registered the sound of her phone ringing but couldn't quite get herself to wake up enough to answer it. She ignored it long enough for it to stop, only to start up again a minute later.

Groaning, she made herself sit up and glanced at the face of the large alarm clock on the side table. It was fifteen after seven in the morning. So much for sleeping in.

She rubbed her eyes, then finally looked at her phone. Mom flashed on the screen. Sedona snatched it up and answered.

"Hello?"

"Oh, thank goodness. I was worried sick when you didn't answer." The words were frantic, but the sound of Mom's voice didn't quite match up.

Sedona rolled her eyes. "I was still asleep, Mom. I'm fine."

"Oh, it's barely seven there, isn't it? Sorry, sweetheart. It's just that your father streamed the news this morning, and we saw the benefit concert and the interview with you and your band. That's wonderful! I'm so sorry we weren't there to see it." There was an actual tone of regret in the sentiment.

"I wish you could've been there." Sedona meant it. "It was an amazing night, and hopefully, enough funds were raised to help with any repairs they might need for the community center."

"It sounds lovely. Maybe the interview will bring the notoriety you and your band need to regain some of the traction you lost."

And there it was.

"Mom, it's not about regaining traction or finding a way to go down the path we've already traveled. It's about finding a new way. One that works for us and our vision. Honestly, I think it's coming together just fine."

Mom gave an exaggerated gasp. "Your dad just came in. I think he'd like to talk to you."

Sedona spent the following ten minutes talking to her dad

about food and the sports events that he'd like to see some-time. Not once did he mention the concert or missing it. "Honey, you be careful and listen to Connor. He'll keep you safe. Love you."

"Love you, too. Bye, Dad."

He hung up, and she set her phone on the side table and let out a low groan. As much as she'd love to be one of those people who could go back to sleep after being awakened like that, she simply wasn't—never had been. And now it was late enough that she likely missed out on the best breakfast options downstairs.

Her thoughts shifted to Mac in the next room, and immediately, her mood lifted. Had he gone down to get breakfast? Was he waiting to eat with her? Did he normally sleep in when he wasn't on assignment like this?

She let herself fall against the pillows. There was no telling what today held, and even though she was nervous about seeing Mac, she still didn't regret those amazing kisses.

Well, there was no sense in lying around and wasting time now that she was awake. Just in case Mac was still asleep, she opted to get ready completely before texting him. She didn't mind waiting around her room until he was ready.

She went through her suitcase and decided today was going to be a good day to get some laundry done before they left for San Antonio. There wouldn't be a whole lot of time once they got there, before they'd need to prepare for the next concert.

Once she'd dressed in a clean pair of jeans and a soft, pale blue, long-sleeved shirt, she turned to the bathroom mirror to tame her hair. Fifteen minutes later, she examined her reflection and nodded with satisfaction.

Sedona got her phone and sent a text to Mac.

I'm awake and ready for the day. Phone call from my mom. No rush. I'm going over some songs.

She barely had time to start working when a low knock came from the main door. Surprised, Sedona left the table and looked through the peephole to find Joel and Chloe standing on the other side.

Her curiosity piqued, she unlocked and opened the door, ushering them both inside. "Hey, guys. Come on in. Is everything okay?"

Chloe gave Joel a sideways look. "Everything will be fine. We just needed to talk to you about a few things before everyone gathers later. I was worried we were going to wake you up."

"No, you're good." Sedona cleared off the table and motioned for them to take the chairs and then sat on the bed. Her mind whirred with possibilities for why Joel, especially, was looking so somber.

He pinned Chloe with a look and gave her a nod.

She pressed her lips together and seemed to be looking for the right words. "We'd like to know what you think about Nick."

Sedona blinked in surprise. She hadn't said a thing about Nick's background to the others. She hadn't said much of anything. Suddenly feeling guilty for not including two of her best friends and bandmates in what was going on outside the essential information, she tempered her reaction.

"He's a talented drummer, and the audience seems to love him. It's been nice to have a dedicated driver, too." Even she was aware of how generic that response was.

Joel gave her a look that encouraged her to elaborate.

Sedona waved at him. "Maybe if you guys told me what was going on, I would know how to better answer the question."

Joel stayed quiet, and finally Chloe sat up straighter, a look of uncertainty on her face.

"Nick came to my room last night. Like, late last night, and wanted to come inside. I told him I was exhausted and suggested we talk this morning at breakfast. Instead of backing off and agreeing, he tried to push past me and get inside anyway. I literally had to put my body between the door and the doorframe to keep him from coming in." She shifted uncomfortably. "It was just weird, you know? He apologized and left. Never did tell me why he wanted to talk in the first place."

"That's really, really weird." Sedona looked from Chloe to Joel.

Chloe folded her arms across her chest. "I just got a strange vibe. I don't know if he wanted to come in because he wanted to talk about you, or if he's developing an interest in me. Although my reaction last night probably put a kibosh on the whole thing if he was."

Joel leaned forward. "Either way, I think we should take this seriously, especially in light of your stalker. I've seen Nick stare at you, Sedona. Like watching you walk across a room, or when you're talking to someone else. I don't know. There's been something off about him for the last couple of months but knowing that he tried to force his way into Chloe's room has me concerned."

Sedona replayed several instances when Nick had gotten in her space since they'd been on tour. "Yeah, I've noticed some things, too. Enough to be a little odd, but not enough to actually make me feel uncomfortable. At least not until now."

A knock came from the connecting door, which drew everyone's attention.

Sedona started to walk that way when Joel put out a hand to stop her.

"Can you ask him to wait until we're done talking? This is between the three of us for right now. I think we should come up with a game plan first before we pull someone else in."

"Yeah. Of course."

Joel and Chloe spoke in a murmur as Sedona opened the connecting door to reveal Mac standing on the other side.

There was a hesitant smile on his face that faded as soon as he saw her company.

He lowered his voice as he studied her face. "Is everything okay?"

"I'm not sure yet. We have an issue with Nick. I'm trying to get to the bottom of it now. I'm sorry, but can I text you once we're done talking?"

Concern darkened his features. "I'll be here if you need anything."

"Thank you."

Both doors closed simultaneously, and she returned to the table where her friends were disagreeing about something.

"If we do that, it'll ruin everything." Chloe sounded irritated. "We need a solid plan, and right now we don't even have proof that Nick's behind any of it. If he is, he can't be working alone. Half of what's happened has been while we were all on stage."

"If we do what?" Sedona reclaimed her spot on the bed.

Chloe waved an impatient hand at Joel. "He thinks we should talk to Nick and ask him to step away from the band. Today."

"Why not? Things have escalated, and if Nick is behind it all, then we should do something sooner rather than later." It was clear Joel thought there was no downside to what he was suggesting.

Sedona shook her head. "I'm not sure that's the way to go. I get what you're saying, but if we do that, it'll put an end to the tour. Without proof, it's like shooting ourselves in the foot. There's no way we'll find another drummer by tonight. Not to mention, if we accuse him, he'll know we're onto him and make a run for it. It'll be really hard to report him then."

"Are you willing to take the risk that Nick is the one who's been messaging you? Because I'm not." Joel planted his feet on the floor and rested his arms on the table. "The fact is, it's always been the three of us. If we have to go back to that and build up again, we'll be fine."

Sedona got his point. And if they were sure it was Nick, she'd be all for not only ending the tour but making sure he got thrown in jail for everything he'd done. The problem was, they *weren't* sure. Not really.

She felt bad for not sharing what they'd learned about Nick and the women who had filed charges against him. She didn't know if it was information she even could.

"I hate to say it, Joel, but I think we need to continue like we are. We've got to catch Nick red-handed or at least have some evidence to prove it's him." She turned to Chloe. "What's your opinion?"

"I'd just hate to kick Nick out of the band just to have the stalker continue to come after you. If it's Nick, let's get proof. And if it isn't, we can wait to let him go until after the tour is over."

"Agreed. For the record, Joel, I think you're right. I think we need to replace Nick with someone else. For now, let's talk to Mac. Make sure he's aware of these new developments."

Joel didn't look happy with her decision, but he tipped his head in acceptance. "Let's do that then. But I want you both to promise me you won't put yourselves in a position where you're alone with Nick. Let's watch out for each other."

"I promise," Chloe spoke up immediately. "Trust me, last night was enough weird from him for a long while."

Sedona pressed her hand to her chest. "I promise."

"All right. I'm going to get out there so we don't look too suspicious, all leaving the room at the same time." He put a hand on her shoulder and another on Chloe's. "I'll see you girls later."

He strode out of the room and closed the door behind him. Sedona immediately locked it again and turned to Chloe. "I'm sorry that was so creepy last night. Are you okay?"

"I'm fine. It was completely unexpected. It was more of an unsettled feeling than it was anything else, know what I mean?" She chewed on the inside of her cheek. "I'm not going to lie. I'm looking forward to Christmas break. I think we all need some downtime without the scary drama."

Sedona couldn't agree more.

A few days ago, she imagined hiding out at her place for a while. She could work on songs, watch Christmas movies on TV until her eyes were bleary, and do some baking. There was no way she could ever eat everything she made, but the treats were always welcome at church by everyone, especially members of the youth group.

Now, she couldn't help but picture Mac sharing some of those simple moments with her. She knew it was foolish—just because they'd shared a few kisses didn't mean they were spending the holidays together. Still, they were kisses she would never forget, and they made her want to hope for a future that seemed impossible.

TWENTY-FIVE

Mac waited a long fifteen minutes until Sedona invited him into her room, where Chloe was waiting. He listened as Chloe told him what happened last night with Nick. It didn't matter what Nick wanted to talk about—he shouldn't have tried to force his way into Chloe's room like that. Sedona mentioned how badly Joel wanted Nick removed from the band. Mac was relieved to hear that they'd be asking him to leave once the tour was over.

In the meantime, both women needed to be careful. If his past interactions with women were true, Mac didn't trust Nick to be a gentleman if they had to tell him to back off and leave them alone.

"Chloe, if something like that happens again, don't hesitate to close the door in his face or step past him into the hall. Whatever it takes to make sure you're not alone with him in your room."

Chloe relaxed slightly, though concern still lingered in her expression. "Do you guys think Nick could be the stalker?"

"I wish we knew for sure. But we'll find out, and whoever the stalker is, he *will* be caught." Mac spoke with a conviction he felt, and he hoped that both women would find some comfort in it.

He focused on Sedona, who gave him an approving nod. Still, there was tension in her face that suggested that she had worries she wasn't willing to say aloud.

Chloe brightened a little. "It's too bad we can't force the stalker's hand. Bait him. You know, like they do on TV." She put her palms together and wiggled her fingers like she was coming up with some brilliant plan.

Mac only half listened as the two ladies joked back and forth about an elaborate and incredibly unrealistic plan to catch the stalker. He enjoyed the easy way the friends interacted. Even more, he liked how Sedona's laugh seemed to wrap itself around his heart.

He'd been looking forward to seeing Sedona this morning but had no idea what to expect. He didn't regret their kisses for a moment. Unfortunately, it complicated things. A lot. He couldn't afford to be distracted. Not when it came to protecting her.

He knew the smart thing would be to put his job first and act as if nothing had happened between them. At the very least, he should make sure it didn't happen again. But the instant he saw her this morning, he experienced an overwhelming sense of belonging, as though being near her felt like home.

He forced himself to focus on the conversation happening in front of him.

Chloe pointed to a plastic laundry bag sitting near the door. "Looks like you're planning to get laundry done today? Same here. Let's make sure we go together."

"Absolutely. I need to find something to eat quickly. I'm starving."

Chloe's eyes widened. "You didn't make it down to the breakfast? Are you okay?"

Sedona chuckled. "I'm fine. I didn't sleep well." Her

cheeks turned pink then, and she seemed to be purposefully avoiding his eyes. "Then my mom forgot about the time difference and called first thing. I'll eat a snack and wait for lunch. I promise I won't starve."

"Okay. I need to get a shower in. How about I text you in about forty-five minutes?"

Sedona checked her watch and nodded. "Sounds good."

He followed the ladies to the door. He and Sedona waited long enough to see that Chloe made it into her room safely.

Mac moved back to the table while Sedona closed and locked the door.

"I think it's wise of you to let Nick go after the tour. It might be a good idea to talk to him and let him know what happened was inappropriate, and that you ladies don't feel comfortable with that kind of behavior."

Sedona slipped her hands into the pockets of her jeans. "You're probably right. He never fit in completely anyway."

The pale blue blouse she wore made her eyes practically glow. She hastily pulled her hair up into a messy bun. Silky tendrils curled near her ears, tempting Mac to reach out and finger one.

He kept his spot near the door. "I think this will be enough to warrant a deep dive into Nick's financials. Like you guys said, if it *is* him, he must be working with someone else, and I doubt that person is doing anything for free. Maybe we can find some evidence of a money trail."

"I hope so." She gathered several items from the bathroom and put them in her suitcase. "Just trying to clean up. That way, as soon as the laundry is done, I can pack it too, and be ready to go. We may not have a performance tonight, but it's nice to get to a new place early enough to get settled."

She'd barely looked at him since Chloe left, and there was no doubt in his mind that she was purposefully trying to stay busy.

As though she realized what she was doing, she paused,

then slowly turned to face him. "I'm sorry. I'm not sure…" She lifted her shoulders slightly, and her cheeks turned a rosy pink.

"I'm not either. You know, if it helps."

"It does. A little."

Mac didn't have any more answers than he did when he woke up that morning, but an understanding passed between them. That would have to be enough for now.

"Why don't I let you work on your packing, and I'll go check in and let Asher or Cole know what's going on. It'd be great if Officer Carrington could get that financial check going as soon as possible. Let me know when you and Chloe are ready, and I'll help you guys down to the laundromat."

"That sounds like a plan. Thank you, Mac."

"You're welcome. Don't forget to eat something, okay?" With a smile, he retreated from the tension to his room and closed the connecting door most of the way. He took in a fortifying breath and let it back out again.

They were going to need to talk about this, because there was no way that at least Chloe wasn't going to pick up on the shift between them.

Which was exactly why he should've kept it professional in the first place.

Unwilling to beat himself up over what already was, he dialed Cole's number and waited for his brother to answer.

"Hey, Mac. How're things going?"

"We've had a couple of new developments. You at The Castle or home?" He looked at the time. Peter should already be at school. Cole regularly dropped him off before coming in to work.

"The Castle. What's up?"

"I spoke with Asher early this morning. Didn't even know if he was awake and functioning yet."

Cole chuckled. "Well, he's awake. I'm not sure how much he's functioning. There were mutters about keeping D&D

games to Fridays and Saturdays from now on, no matter what time of year it is."

"We'll see if he remembers that next time." Mac laughed because they both knew all too well that Asher would make the same mistake again.

"Exactly. Okay, so what's going on?"

Mac told him about Nick and what happened last night with Chloe. He also shared how Joel had wanted Nick gone now, but that the women had convinced him to wait until after the tour. "There may be some tension going forward. I'm not sure how well Joel, or Chloe for that matter, is going to do at keeping it cool. If Nick is the guy, this might be the push he needs to escalate. If we can dive into his financials and see if there are any red flags…"

"… then it might give us some proof and maybe even lead us to the person he's working with, since there's no way he could've pulled it all off on his own. Yep, we'll get on it. As soon as I hang up, either Asher or I will contact Officer Carrington and see if they can get a warrant to get that information."

"I appreciate it. Did Dad have a chance to talk to Truitt yet about that job?"

"Not yet, but he was planning to do that today. I'll let you know how it goes. Truitt always said he wanted to be a US Marshal. I don't know if that's still the plan or not. It'd be nice to bring someone else in, though."

"Yeah, it would." Mac's thoughts drifted to Sedona.

The fact was, they had enough business to keep them all busy right now. Bringing in another person or two would give everyone a little more room to be flexible like if Mac needed to make regular trips to the DFW area to visit a certain music artist.

"Hey, Cole? You got a minute for video? Preferably where we can talk and keep this between the two of us."

"Hold on. Okay, I'm in the gym." A moment later, Cole's voice came on screen. "What's up?"

Mac wasn't one to bring up personal issues, except that Cole had gone through a very similar situation recently with Erica. If he could offer some insight, especially when Mac wasn't sure what to do, it would be worth it. He moved into the bathroom and closed the door.

"I need your advice from the viewpoint of providing private security and then… having feelings for the woman you're supposed to be protecting."

Cole's brows rose. "Okay, first things first. I feel like I do need to ask: Are the feelings mutual?"

"I think so. Or at least, I feel like they could be. The problem is, we're both doing what we're supposed to do when it comes to our careers, you know? I'm not sure how we could realistically bridge the gap. And as old-fashioned as it sounds, I'm not willing to start a relationship that doesn't have a future. I've been there before, and I won't make the same mistake again."

"First of all, the situation with Cassie was different. She wasn't honest with you from the start. She knew what you did for a living and what that meant before you got married. I don't know Sedona well at all, but I can say that she's clearly nothing like Cassie. It's not fair to compare the two."

"No, you're right." Mac ran a hand across the back of his neck. "The last thing I want to do is put Sedona in danger because I allow myself to be distracted from the real reason I'm here. Enough has happened, though, that I can't just pretend it didn't."

"I was there with Erica. Even though it doesn't seem like it at the time, things have a way of working out. With us, it was totally a God thing. I mean, He somehow managed to work out my relationship with her and help me let go of the anger I'd been fighting. All at the same time." Cole shrugged. "I know our situations are different because Sedona hired you to protect her. Take what you feel for her and hone it to focus on keeping her safe. It doesn't have to distract you from your job. It can make you even better at it. Trust me, there's a primal need to protect the woman you love."

Mac laughed nervously. "Well, I think it's a bit early to go that far, but I get what you're saying." The funny thing was, he could easily see himself falling for Sedona. He was halfway there already.

"In the meantime, pray about it. I'll do the same. If you and Sedona are meant to be together, things will work out eventually."

It was hard for Mac to imagine that, at least right now. But Cole was right, God had a hand in Cole's life and his marriage to Erica. Mac liked to think God might have a plan for him, too.

"You're surprisingly good at this whole advice thing. I expect you to keep that compliment between the two of us."

Cole tipped his head back and laughed loudly. "Your secret is safe with me, though I should have recorded this conversation for proof. Or blackmail if the need arises."

"Yeah, I'm glad you didn't." He re-opened the bathroom door so he could hear Sedona if she needed anything. "Back on topic. If we can't catch this guy before the end of the tour, then we're going to have to talk about what to do. I can't, in good conscience, walk away from her and leave her dealing with this stalker."

He'd take a vacation and help her on his own time before he'd do that.

"Agreed. We'll cross that bridge when we come to it."

TWENTY-SIX

The rest of the morning flew by. Everyone got laundry done before they all checked out of the hotel. They drove to a small grocery store to stock up on lunch supplies and snacks. In the parking lot, they checked the tires on the van and trailer, then made sandwiches to eat as they started their drive to San Antonio.

Sedona was more than ready to tackle hers as soon as she got buckled in.

Lou spoke up from the seat behind her. "I always said that sandwiches taste better when you're on the road or after a day in the sun. I still maintain that's true, but it might be a while before I eat another one once we get back home."

"Hear, hear." Nick merged onto the highway and took a bite of his.

Right now, Sedona was so hungry that hers tasted great. But overall, she had to agree with them. It's not like they ate sandwiches for every lunch over the last five weeks, but it was at least three out of four times.

"They're a great way to save time and money, though." Mac opened a bag of barbecue chips. "Can't argue with the portability, either."

Chloe chuckled. "I take it sandwiches are a staple when it comes to private security."

"Yep."

"Yep."

Connor and Mac echoed each other, resulting in laughter from everyone else.

Mac's laugh, which had a deep and rich tone, warmed Sedona's heart. She glanced at him and earned herself a slight wink in response.

There'd barely been time to get everything done this morning. There definitely hadn't been time to talk just the two of them. She knew they needed to and sensed there were things Mac wanted to say.

Would he apologize for initiating their kiss? Would he promise not to cross that line again?

Both responses would be perfectly logical. After all, they'd only known each other for a week, and things had been tense. It wasn't exactly the ideal circumstance to meet someone. Not to mention, they didn't even live in the same town. Realistically, it was hard to see how a relationship could possibly work.

Yet, she had no doubt that if whatever was between them ended before they ever had a chance to begin, she'd always wonder if things could've been different.

That intense need to do something bubbled up in her chest. Nothing was going to be figured out now, though. She focused on her food and listened as Nick muttered through the Houston traffic.

By that point, the lack of sleep last night was catching up with Sedona. She grabbed her jacket from the floorboard, balled it up, and used it as a pillow as she leaned against the window.

The next thing she knew, Joel was shaking her shoulder. "Wake up, sleeping beauty."

She rarely slept in a moving vehicle. Disoriented, she sat

upright and looked out the window at a gas station. "Where are we?"

Lou slid the van door open. "San Antonio. You slept the whole way." He chuckled, and Joel joined him.

Chloe leaned over the seat. "Just ignore them. We're in Brookshire. You did sleep for over an hour, though."

Apparently, she needed it more than she realized. Sedona just hated the groggy feeling after a nap. She tried to shake it off and reached for her bag on the floorboard.

Mac was standing outside the van. He offered a hand to Chloe and helped her out and then did the same for Sedona. It was such a simple kindness, yet when her hand slid into his, every nerve seemed to fire. His thumb brushed the top of her hand right before he released it.

Nick topped off the gas tank while the rest of them walked into the gas station. Fifteen minutes later, everyone had some kind of snack, and they continued their drive.

Sedona took the first nibble of her Heath bar. The combination of chocolate and toffee was exactly what she needed, and the sugar rush didn't hurt either.

Except for the music playing on the radio, the van was quiet as everyone focused on their snack and then found something to occupy their time.

Even if she hadn't been paying attention, she would've known when they reached San Antonio by the increase in Nick's mutterings. They managed to find their way to the downtown area and their hotel, which was right on the River Walk, not ten minutes from the venue where they would be performing in a few short hours. It was too bad they didn't have more time. She would've liked the chance to see the River Walk with all the Christmas lights

"You know," Lou said as they pulled into the hotel parking lot and maneuvered to the area in front of the main doors, "until I first visited San Antonio myself, I always thought of the movie *Cloak & Dagger* every time I saw pictures of the River Walk."

Nick looked at him in the rearview mirror. "I'm not sure I've ever seen that one."

"It's from the 1980s. A thriller about a boy who gets caught up with a bunch of spies." Lou released his seat belt so he could get them checked in. "He runs through San Antonio, and there are a lot of familiar places if you've been here before. Including the Alamo and the River Walk."

Mac reached over to open the van door so Lou could get out. "It's a great movie. Worth watching if you haven't seen it before. Those kinds of movies always made Livi nervous when she was little. She scared easily, and having someone sneak up on her during a tense scene didn't help matters." He chuckled.

"The joys of having older brothers, huh?" Chloe held a hand to her chest in mock pain. "Mine loved to torture me every chance he had."

"Older sisters have their own forms of torture, trust me." Connor got out of the van and stretched.

Sedona enjoyed hearing all the sibling rivalry stories, and they made her laugh, but they also left her wishing she had similar stories to share.

One thing was certain: when she got married, she wanted at least two kids, even if it meant adopting the second one. Although being thirty-two, she was starting to wonder whether any of that was in the cards for her. A possibility that her mom liked to point out on a regular basis.

Sometimes she wondered why her parents even cared. They weren't hands-on with their own daughter. She had a difficult time picturing them doting on a grandchild.

Sedona would be different. Her kids would know how important they were to her and how much she loved them. She'd make plenty of other mistakes, but they would never doubt how much they were wanted.

Tears flooded her eyes, and she quickly turned her attention to the window on her side of the van.

Her cell phone pinged with a text. A glance at the screen showed it was from Mac. Without looking at him, Sedona swiped to read it.

Hey, Sunshine. Are you okay?

His use of the nickname he'd called her last night immediately brought back the intensity of their kisses, and even more than that, the feeling of being completely safe while being held in his arms.

It's a long story. I'll be fine, just need to get out of my own head.

She felt his gaze as she put way more effort than necessary into making sure she had everything in her bag. Thankfully, it didn't take long for Lou to return. They parked the van and trailer, then gathered their luggage and headed inside.

Mac shouldered his bag and reached for her rolling suitcase. "Here, let me take that one for you." His fingers brushed hers as she relinquished the handle, leaving her to carry her purse and guitar case.

"We're on the second floor," Lou was telling them as they piled into the elevator. "We have connecting rooms again. They were the only two hotels with them, and again, I was originally thinking of Sedona and Chloe." He flashed an apologetic look.

Sedona was just as glad, though. She liked the layout in Houston and was thankful they'd have a similar one here.

They got their assignments figured out and agreed to meet for dinner in an hour and then head for the venue from there. Everyone disappeared into their rooms, leaving Mac and Sedona in the hallway.

She swiped her key card and was rewarded with a green light. She pushed the door open and went inside. Mac flipped a light on as he followed her. He set her suitcase on the small dresser and rested the door wedge against the wall.

"You know, even with a mom and sister, I still haven't mastered knowing when I'm supposed to accept that a woman is fine or when I should try to help make her feel better." He set his duffel bag on the floor. "So how about this? If you ever want to talk, I'm here."

"I appreciate it. Truly, I do. There was a whole thought process that got me to where I was, and it ended with a hypothetical family situation that I'm not sure our friendship is quite ready for."

"First of all, I like being your friend, and I take that responsibility seriously. Also, now you've got me curious." He plopped down in a chair at the little table, then clasped his hands together like he was ready to sit and listen to anything she had to say.

It was cute.

She gave her head a subtle shake but couldn't keep from smiling. "Ask me about it again some other time."

One eyebrow rose as he leaned back in the chair. "I'll do that."

Mac's phone rang, and he took it out of his pocket. "Saved by the ring," he told her with a wink before swiping to answer it. "Hey, Asher." He listened for a moment. "Sedona's here with me. One second, and I'll put you on speaker."

He did and set the phone in the middle of the table. Sedona pulled up a chair.

"Okay, we're both here," Mac told him.

"Hey, Sedona. Good luck at your concert tonight."

"Thanks, Asher. I appreciate that."

"All right, Logan and I have been working together today, and we got Nick's financials back. We didn't find any indication of large sums of money coming or going from his bank account. If he *is* the stalker or working with him, then he's being subtle about giving or accepting payment. In other words, we've found nothing to insinuate he's connected to the threats against you."

That should've been good news. At this point, Sedona wasn't a big fan of the guy. But there was a big difference between strongly disliking his personality and his past, and him being a stalker who was threatening to hurt her.

"Now, we did have some luck on the burner phone that this guy's been using to contact you. Or phones, I should say. It turns out the first bunch of texts you got from him—the ones you received before you reached out to Durham Private Security—were all sent from the same phone. The one in Austin was sent from a different phone, and then again, a different one last night. I wonder if it's a coincidence that he first changed phones after Mac joined you all, or if he simply decided to do so more regularly to make sure he doesn't get caught. Either way, the timing is interesting."

Mac leaned forward. "It's interesting because, if he did change his pattern because I showed up on the scene, it means he knows who I am and is keeping a close eye on all of us."

"Exactly."

"That's incredibly disconcerting." Sedona wasn't sure she liked this new information. The idea that this person had been listening to their conversations brought a whole new level of ick that made her uneasy. Even more so if it was Nick, because he'd been right there the whole time.

"Now, we do have an idea we're working on. Since we know this guy likely ditched his old phone and bought at least one new phone in Destiny. Logan and I found the gas stations near where your hotel was, Sedona, as well as the concert locations, then cross-referenced those places with their sale records and came up with one store that sold three burner phones to the same individual the day after you were officially hired, Mac."

"Wow." Sedona was seriously impressed. "I never would've thought to do all of that. Seems like it would be some crazy coincidence if this guy isn't the stalker."

"Agreed." Mac reached across the table and covered her hand with his. "Is there any chance you were also able to figure out who bought them?"

"He paid cash. However, the gas station does have a security system. The problem is, the owner refuses to hand over the tapes without a warrant. Officer Carrington is working to get that now. As it is, it'll almost certainly be tomorrow before it comes in, they can seize the video, and we can find that clip."

Sedona tried not to get her hopes up, but it sounded promising. She shifted her hand, allowing Mac's fingers to intertwine gently with hers. "Still, it's way more than we've had up to this point. Thank you, Asher."

"You're welcome. You guys be careful, and as soon as we find anything, I'll give you a call."

"Will do. Thanks, man. Have a good night." Mac ended the call. He ran his thumb over the top of hers. "If this pans out, it could mean we might know who it is and have him in custody before we even get to Dallas tomorrow."

"I hope and pray that's the case." Sedona focused on the feel of her hand nestled in his. "Look, about earlier…"

Her phone rang then, and she gave Mac an apologetic smile as she got it out. "It's Chloe." Reluctantly, she pulled her hand free and answered the call. "Hey, what's up?"

"I was getting my outfit ready for tonight, and I'm having a slight wardrobe malfunction here. Do you have that sewing kit with you? Or is it in the van?"

"I have it here. Give me five minutes, and I'll bring it over." Sedona ended the call and laughed dryly. "Well, earlier will have to wait until later." She stood.

Mac got to his feet and rounded the table and stopped when the toes of his shoes nearly touched the toes of hers. "I'm looking forward to that conversation. I know there's a lot we need to talk about."

His nearness caused all rational thought to flee. Why couldn't she think of anything to say?

"I'd really like to kiss you again. In fact, I've been thinking about it pretty much all day. Do you have any objections?"

She smiled softly as her heart fluttered. "None."

"Good." He touched her lips softly, once and then again, before wrapping her in his embrace. This time, he deepened the kiss with an unhurried sweetness.

When they parted, his gaze lingered on her, warm and intense, as if she were the only person who mattered to him in that moment.

"I'd better escort you over to Chloe's before she wonders what happened to you."

TWENTY-SEVEN

The city looked so peaceful. Quiet. Carefree. There were still plenty of people walking around on the streets below, but from Sedona's hotel room, she couldn't hear the noise. Instead, she soaked in the Christmas lights that were strung on trees, the fronts of businesses, and even along some of the pathways. It was like a Christmas wonderland down there.

Even though she still hadn't had the chance to explore the River Walk, the venue they had their concert at was an amazing close second. The whole place was decorated like a giant living room with a Christmas tree, roaring fireplace, couches, and a rug. The audience was large, but it still felt somehow intimate. As though she was singing in front of family. Even better, the whole performance went off without a hitch.

She was exhausted but happy. Even if they didn't do an official Christmas tour again next year, she wanted to hold a Christmas-themed concert in Dallas at least. Maybe Destiny, too.

Sedona looked over her shoulder at Mac, who was speaking on his phone on the other side of the room. She only heard snippets of the conversation and didn't try to follow it. They were going back to Dallas tomorrow. He'd mentioned possibly arranging for someone else from Durham Private Security to meet them there for the last two concerts.

The good thing about Dallas was that she wouldn't have to stay at a hotel. The idea of sleeping in her own bed sounded amazing.

But then, what would Mac do for sleeping arrangements? Would he stay in a hotel until the tour was over? She'd miss having him so close by if he did. Had he been serious the other day when he said he would stick around even after the last concert if they hadn't caught the stalker?

Because right now, with just a few days left in the tour, it was becoming a real possibility.

Whatever happened, Mac would eventually go home to Destiny. The reality of that hit hard tonight.

"Hey, you."

Sedona jumped. She hadn't even heard the phone conversation end much less Mac approaching.

He chuckled from behind her and placed his hands on her shoulders. "I didn't mean to scare you." His arms went around her waist, and she leaned into his solid chest. "What're you thinking about?"

Sedona pointed to an especially colorful light display across the street from the hotel. "Aren't all the lights pretty?"

"They sure are." He nuzzled her ear and then hugged her close.

"Someday, my house is going to be one of those that's just covered in lights and decorations. People will either come from all over town to see it, or it'll be labeled tacky and avoided at all costs. Either way, I'll be okay with it."

He laughed, and she felt the vibrations against her back. "Sunshine, I don't doubt one bit that you'll do exactly that."

They stood in silence for several minutes, and Sedona enjoyed the feel of his arms around her.

"It'll be nice to get home tomorrow," she began, "but it feels a bit like the end of something else."

"Like when you go home after summer camp. You want to see your parents, watch TV, play video games, actually get some sleep, and eat your normal food. At the same time, leaving summer camp means leaving something exciting behind and going back to real life again."

"Exactly. I'm not going to miss the hotels. But this…"

Mac's arms tightened around her. "I'm not going to pretend I know what the future holds, and things are complicated right now, but I happen to like *this*. I'd really like the opportunity to stroll through a Christmas light display together or watch a Christmas movie. I'll have some time off once this is all finished. I thought I might spend it in Dallas, if that's okay with you."

Contentment bubbled up in her chest as she turned in his arms and looked up at him. "I'd like that."

He lowered his head and placed a gentle, heartfelt kiss on the corner of her mouth before shifting and covering her lips with his. The tenderness of the moment made her want to melt in his arms.

With one hand, Mac cupped the back of her head, his fingers tangling in her hair. "I don't know what it's going to look like yet, but we're only four hours apart. It could be so much worse. I think what we have is worth exploring."

"So do I."

A slow smile brightened his face. "I happen to recall a conversation we tried to have earlier today. Something you thought our friendship might not quite be far enough along to handle…"

Color crept into her cheeks. He laughed softly, his tone low, and the blush deepened.

"You are so beautiful, Sedona Reeves. I like being able to make you blush."

This time, she swatted his arm and rested her forehead against his chest in embarrassment.

He chuckled again but quickly sobered. "Seriously, though, what was it?"

"Everyone was talking about their siblings while we were driving up here today. Sharing about how their brothers or sisters teased them. It got me thinking about how, once I was married, I'd like to have at least two kids, even if it meant having to adopt." She shrugged and looked up. "It just hit me hard then, I guess."

She'd half expected him to find it funny or to think the conversation was a little presumptuous. To be fair, though, he was the one who insisted she share what she'd been thinking. Instead, his expression held understanding and affection.

"I've got five siblings, and I can't imagine going through life without any of them. I'm with you there—at least two kids are mandatory."

He'd just pressed a kiss to her forehead when the lights winked out, plunging them into darkness.

"Mac?"

He grasped her hand in his. There was a rustling sound, and a moment later, a light turned on, revealing a pocket-sized flashlight in his other hand.

He stepped closer to the window, pulled the curtains back, and looked out.

"Lights are on everywhere else, which means it's just our hotel that's lost power."

"That's a little weird, right?"

"Yeah, it is. Let's give it a minute or two to turn back on." He gave her hand a squeeze. "I've got another flashlight in my bag."

He led her to his room, where he pulled a much larger flashlight from a side pocket in his duffel bag. Once on, it illuminated the room. "Take this one and hold onto it in case you need it." He switched off the small flashlight and pressed it into her hand.

Sedona slipped it into the shallow pocket of her pants. "It's a good thing most people have cell phones these days." She pointed at the clock sitting on his side table, which was currently blank. "All I can think about is a *Home Alone* situation where people wake up tomorrow morning after the power comes back on and their clocks have been reset."

"Great movie. They'd have to change a lot to make it believable now, though." He took his phone out. "I'll call down to the front desk and see what's going on."

The words barely left his mouth when an alarm pierced the air, and a red light started flashing high on the wall.

Sedona's heart lodged in her throat. "Is the building on fire?"

"I don't know." Mac's demeanor shifted in an instant, his focus sharpening as he moved into protective mode. "We can't risk staying if it is, but we're not going to go blindly running down the hallway either."

A banging noise came from Sedona's room, causing her to jump. Mac squeezed her hand.

"I think someone's knocking on my door." She pulled him in that direction. "What if it's Chloe or Joel or someone else from the band?"

He went with her, but when they got to the door, he stopped her from answering it. "Let me check first." He looked through the peephole, opened the door, and stepped back to let Joel inside before closing it again.

Joel nodded his thanks, then faced Sedona. "Is Chloe here?"

"No, I haven't seen her yet." She looked from Joel to Mac and explained. "She was in a house fire when she was a kid. She's got to be terrified."

"I haven't been able to find her. I came here first hoping she'd already been by." Joel pointed at the door. "We need to get to her before she panics. Then we'll worry about meeting up with the others."

Mac pointed his light in their direction. "You both stay in here. I'll go get her and be right back. Seriously, don't let anyone else in unless you hear my voice." He nodded to Sedona. "You have that other flashlight?"

She got it out and turned it on. "Got it. Please be careful."

The moment he left the room, Joel whirled to face Sedona. "I want you to come with me. Let's get out of here and somewhere safe."

Confused, she shook her head.

"No, we need to wait for Mac and Chloe. I don't want to lose them in the chaos. Especially if this isn't an actual fire, and the stalker is trying to draw us out."

"And that's exactly why you should come with me. He'll be expecting you to stay close to Mac. You and I can disappear in the crowd. I'll keep you safe, Sedona." He cupped her face with his palms. "I promise. You just need to trust me."

He took her hand and tried to pull her toward the connecting doors. Her initial hesitation about leaving Mac behind swiftly gave way to panic. She dug her heels in and tried to pull away.

Joel tightened his grip and jerked her close, sending pain shooting through her wrist. As he spun around to look at her, the flashlight caught a fierce anger burning in his eyes. Between that and the harsh shadows, he looked menacing.

"Stop! Joel, you're hurting me."

To her horror, he whipped a gun from the waistband of his pants and pressed it hard into her side. He shoved her through the connecting doors into Mac's room, then locked it behind them.

The muzzle of his gun pressed harder into her ribs and made her cry out in pain. He grabbed the hair on the back of her head and directed her to the door leading to the hallway.

"When I say so, we're going out into the hallway and to

the right." He moved so his mouth was next to her ear. "If you scream or try to get away, I *will* shoot you. Then I'm going to go after Chloe and Mac." His breath, hot against her skin, made fear ripple through her body.

With another harsh tug on her hair, tears welled up and cascaded down her cheeks.

He tightened his grip on her hair. "Do you understand?"

"Yes. I understand."

The words barely left her lips when someone pounded on the connecting door.

"Sedona?" Mac's voice competed with the continued resonance of the alarm.

"Now. Go."

Joel reached around her to pull the door open, then shoved her into the hallway where other people were running for the stairwell.

That's where Sedona thought they'd be going. Instead, he passed it at a run, then used a key card to open another door. She noticed it was room 210 as he all but threw her inside. He slid the locks in place, snatched the flashlight from her, and motioned to the bed.

"Sit down."

Her stomach churned as she backed up until her legs hit the edge of the bed. She nearly fell but caught herself just in time.

"Why are you doing this?" Even now, Sedona had a hard time reconciling that he was the one behind it all. She'd known him for years, and never once had she thought he'd be capable of this kind of violence.

Suddenly, completely unconcerned about anything else, he got a chair and moved it to face the bed a good eight feet away. He took a seat and kept the gun and flashlight pointed at her.

"You were too selfish. Too self-involved to see how much I love you." The words flew out of his mouth with a vehemence that made her jump. "All I wanted was for us to be together. You should've taken that record deal, Sedona, and sent Chloe packing. It would've been just the two of us topping charts and living the dream."

The weird lighting and shadows on his face, combined with his raw anger, made him seem more like a figure from a terrifying dream than the man she thought she knew.

"I had no idea, Joel. You never told me. Never gave any indication that you felt that way about me." Sedona tried to think of a time when he showed her preference over Chloe. Maybe subtly at times. He was always open to hanging out when they had time, whether Chloe was there or not. He'd never done something she would've considered inappropriate.

"I stuck by your side, didn't I? Even when you walked away from a sweet payday with Moonlight Studios. I've given you friendship. I've made sure you never spent a birthday or Christmas alone. I was there for you, Sedona, like no other man has ever been." Joel put his elbows on his knees and leaned forward, his gun still aimed at her chest. "I kept waiting for you to see me. To see what we have together."

The flashlight was still shining on her face, and the brightness made her eyes burn. She squeezed them shut. *Please, God, get me out of this. Help me know what to do. Help Mac find me.*

TWENTY-EIGHT

The fire alarms continued, the piercing sound giving Sedona a headache. She lifted a hand to shield her eyes from the light. "If only you'd said something… You could've told me how you felt about me."

"I shouldn't have had to." Joel spat out.

"So why all the threatening messages? If you love me, then why would you scare me like that?"

She had no idea how much time had passed since they'd disappeared into the hallway. Was Mac out there looking for her? He'd probably think they left the building. How would he know to look for her here?

Her cell phone was in her back pocket, but right now, Joel was watching her. There was no way she could get it out and call for help without him seeing it. And if Joel took it away…

The anger on his face shifted to sorrow so quickly it was creepy. "I wanted you to see that I could protect you. That I could keep you safe. Even after Connor got here, I knew he wouldn't stand in our way."

He launched to his feet. The beam of the flashlight bounced around the room as he drew closer. Wrath replaced the sorrow on his face, and it made Sedona's skin crawl.

"Then, instead of relying on me, you hired that guy who has no idea how to take care of you. Not like I do."

Joel's connection with reality was unraveling, and Sedona sensed her time was running out. She had to make him think she was coming around—anything to get him to lower that gun.

"You don't understand." She stood slowly and held her hands out in front of her. "I hired Mac to protect us all. I thought the stalker was real, and I didn't want you or Chloe to get hurt, either."

"I'm not stupid, Sedona. I've seen the way you look at him. It's the way you should've been looking at me."

She took a tentative step forward. "Please, put the gun down. We can talk about this and figure out what to do next."

With no warning, he backhanded her across the face. The force of it knocked her onto the bed as pain ricocheted through her head, and the metallic taste of blood filled her mouth. Tears stung her eyes.

"It's too late for that now."

Sedona swiped the back of her hand across her chin where blood ran from her mouth and upper lip. She was still half lying on the bed where she'd fallen. As discreetly as possible, she eased the phone from her back pocket, then moved to sit up again with her leg covering it.

Joel shone the flashlight on her face, winced, and quickly aimed it back down on the floor. "If you'd only realized we were supposed to be together, then none of this would've happened."

Blood went down the back of her throat, making her cough. With nothing else to use, she pulled her sleeve up over her hand and held it against the cut on her lip. There was little she could do for the one on the inside of her cheek.

She focused on the phone beneath her leg. She didn't dare turn it on. The screen would light up like a spotlight in the dark room, and then Joel would take away her one chance to call for help.

When Joel brought her into the room, she'd noticed the room number. At the first chance, she'd send it to Mac and pray he found her in time.

The moment Mac walked back into Sedona's room, only to find both she and Joel were gone, a ball of lead settled in the pit of his stomach. He walked over to the connecting doors and knocked hard. "Sedona?" He couldn't imagine why they would've gone next door, but it was better than the alternative possibilities he was sorting through in his head.

"What's going on?" Connor spoke up from behind him.

Mac whirled to face him, Chloe, and Nick, whom he'd found in the hallway on their way over. "I left Sedona and Joel here, but now they're gone." He addressed Connor directly. "The three of you check Lou's room. I'm going to go next door and make sure everything's okay."

Connor held up his flashlight. "We've got it."

Mac jogged past them, out into the hallway, and to the door leading to his room. He swiped his card and pushed it open.

No one.

They'd pretty much ruled Joel out as the stalker in the beginning because Sedona and Chloe had known him for so long. But the truth was, he had just as much opportunity to torment Sedona as anyone else did, not to mention he had a bigger emotional investment.

Mac had left Sedona with the very man who'd been after her all this time.

He felt a blaze of anger at Joel, but he was also deeply disappointed in himself. He never should've left her. Period. Blaming himself wouldn't help—he could do that once

Sedona was safe. For now, he had to focus and use his anger as fuel to do whatever it took to find her.

He burst into the hallway and nearly ran into Chloe and the others, including Lou.

Mac spoke quickly. "Joel took Sedona. I believe he's the stalker."

"What?" Chloe shook her head. "I don't believe it. Why would he do that?"

"I don't know. Connor, I need you to go downstairs. See if you can find a manager with a master key and bring him back to this floor. Chloe, call the police and let them know Sedona's missing and that Joel's the suspect. Tell them she's in imminent danger. Nick, you and Lou go to the first floor and keep an eye on the exits. Make sure Joel doesn't try to take Sedona out of the building in the chaos."

"I'll be back as quickly as possible," Connor told him. The group jogged away from Mac and disappeared into the stairwell, Chloe already dialing her phone.

The hotel was a monstrosity with ten floors total. Joel could have Sedona anywhere. The problem was that, until Mac got that master key, he couldn't even start searching the rooms.

He couldn't think about Joel harming Sedona. He had to stay focused

"Father God, please watch over Sedona and keep her safe. Help me find her, so I can help her get out of this in one piece."

To his relief, he waited barely five minutes before a bouncing light against the wall at the end of the hallway announced Connor's return. He jogged toward Mac, a key card held in his hand.

"I've got the master." He handed it to Mac. "The manager should be sending someone down to flip the breaker. See if we can get the lights back on. So far, there's no sign of smoke or a fire, but the fire department is on the way. Chloe said the police will be here soon, too."

"Good. Let's check Joel's room first. Then we're going to have to go room by room after that. Joel planned this way ahead of time. He could have another key card or may have even stolen a master. We have to assume he could be in any of these rooms. Are you carrying?" Mac took some comfort in the weight of his own handgun holstered beneath his waistband.

"Yep." Connor patted his waist. "Let's start on this floor and work our way up. With the others watching the first floor, there's no way Joel's going to risk leaving a room there to bring her back upstairs."

"Agreed."

The lights flickered on, and Mac flinched against the brightness. He turned his flashlight off, clipped it to his belt, and withdrew his gun.

At Joel's room, Connor withdrew his gun as well. Mac swiped the card, waited for the light to turn green, then nodded to Connor, who turned the handle and shoved the door open. He stayed in the doorway while Mac quickly scanned the room.

There was no sign of Joel or Sedona.

Together, the men cleared several more rooms, and each of them was empty. With each step down the hallway, Mac did his best to push aside the growing anxiety gnawing at him.

What if they were wrong, and Joel had managed to get Sedona out of the building? They could be anywhere by now if that were the case.

Mac's phone pinged with a text. His eyes widened when he checked it and saw Sedona's name. He swiped to a three-digit number.

"That's my girl," he murmured with satisfaction as he jammed the phone into his back pocket. "They're in room 210.

When I go in, I'm hoping we'll have the element of surprise. But I'd like you to hang back in case that's not enough."

"Understood."

They quickly progressed down the hallway and stopped in front of the room they were looking for.

Mac got ready, gave Connor a nod, and then swiped the card. The moment the green light came on and the door clicked, he knew Joel would have been alerted.

Without hesitating, Mac shoved the door open and stepped inside, his gun raised.

Joel stood at the opposite end of the room, his left hand clamped onto Sedona's hair at the back of her head to keep her in place in front of him, a gun pressed to her ribs. Blood covered her mouth and dripped down her chin.

Mac clenched his jaw, the tendons in his neck tightening.

Joel sneered. "Don't try to be a hero. If you take one more step, I'll pull this trigger." He jabbed the gun, and Sedona cried out.

"I guarantee if you shoot her, you won't make it out of here alive. The only way that's going to happen is if you let her go. Now."

TWENTY-NINE

Sedona's eyes watered as Joel used her hair to hold her in front of him like a shield. Her instant relief at seeing Mac burst through the door was immediately replaced with dread. Fear gripped her—not just for herself, but for Mac. What if Joel shifted his aim and decided to focus his anger on him instead?

"I'm not letting her go." Joel raged.

"Please, Joel." Sedona reached up with her left hand and gripped his wrist where it was holding her hair, hoping for some relief from the constant pulling.

Surprisingly, his grasp on her hair loosened slightly. Whether it was because he felt bad for hurting her or because he was distracted by his confrontation with Mac, she couldn't tell.

Mac kept his gun trained on Joel. "You've obviously got the upper hand here." He slowly took two steps to his left. "You can be the hero in this scenario by doing the right thing and letting Sedona go."

Now that Mac had moved, Sedona noticed the hotel room door hadn't closed completely. A shadow shifted in the crack that revealed the hallway outside. Someone else was out there. She looked at Mac who took another two steps to his left. He caught her eye, his gaze flicking from her to the floor.

He wanted her to drop. But when?

Joel loosened his grip on her hair a little more as he turned slightly to continue facing Mac. "Stop moving!"

Mac ignored him and took another step. Sedona could feel the rage in Joel as he realized Mac had no intention of doing as he asked. Joel's hand shook. He removed the gun from her ribs and swung it around to point it at Mac.

She immediately lifted her feet out from under her, causing herself to fall downward and pull Joel along with her.

The deafening crack of gunfire shattered the tense atmosphere as Joel squeezed the trigger. Mac unleashed his own shot.

Sedona felt Joel stumble. Instead of dropping his weapon, he lifted it again.

Motion in the doorway caught her attention as Connor pushed his way into the room, leveled his gun at Joel, and fired.

Joel slumped to the ground, his grip on her hair going slack. She fell forward and caught herself with her hands as a sob escaped her chest.

Strong arms surrounded her, and the next thing she knew, she was being lifted into the air and gently placed on the bed. Mac knelt in front of her.

"Are you okay?"

Her eyes immediately went to the sleeve of his shirt where blood was beginning to seep through the fabric. "He shot you!"

"Look at me, Sedona. Did he hurt you?" His implication was clear.

She shook her head, the movement causing pain in her head and making her stomach roll with nausea. "No. Not like that."

"Thank God." He moved to sit on the bed beside her and

cradled her in his arms. She soaked in his strength and warmth as the reality that they'd survived finally started to sink in.

Connor was on the floor beside Joel. He'd grabbed a towel and was pressing it to one of the wounds while he spoke on the phone. "We need an ambulance immediately. We've got one gunshot victim and other injuries as well." He told them the hotel and room number before tossing the phone down onto the floor. "He's still alive," he announced as his gaze cut to them. "Are you two okay?"

"I am, thanks to both of you, but Mac needs to go to the hospital." She grabbed a pillowcase and used it to try to stop the flow of blood.

Mac lifted his arm to get a look at the wound through the tear in his shirt. "It just grazed me. I'll be fine." He offered Connor a respectful nod. "Thanks for stepping in."

Connor gave him a nod in return.

Mac's eyes darkened with concern as he gently brushed his thumb over Sedona's bruised lip, his jaw set as he pressed a tender kiss on her forehead.

He stood then and strode across the room to prop the hotel door open. Moments later, police arrived to make sure the scene was contained. Soon after, firefighters and EMTs flooded the room.

The place was chaos as officers tried to sort through what had happened, weapons were confiscated, and everyone was evacuated from the building. As suspected, there never was a fire. As Sedona climbed carefully into the back of an ambulance, she wondered how long Joel had been planning the whole thing.

Sedona was freezing. The nurse spread a warm blanket over her lap and assured her that it was the drain of adrenaline after everything that had happened. That might be mostly true, but seriously, the hospital air was just cold.

"Do you think she'd bring me one, too, if I asked?" Chloe pulled her jacket in tighter. "I'll bet no one gets a residual illness in here because they freeze the bacteria before they have a chance to infect anyone."

Sedona chuckled, then groaned as the stitches in her upper lip pulled taut. The doctor had applied an anesthetic to the wound before placing the two stitches, but it was quickly wearing off. Thankfully, she'd been assured that scarring would be minimal.

The wound on the inside of her mouth was more painful. Her teeth had cut her cheek when Joel had backhanded her. It didn't require stitches, but the doctor told her it'd feel like a canker sore on steroids. She didn't look forward to the next week or so as it healed.

Aside from those wounds and some bruising on the side of her face, she'd been given a clean bill of health.

Which was great, except she wanted to see Mac, who was being treated in a different room. He said the bullet had just grazed his arm, but she'd feel better if she could see that for herself.

Chloe's eyes glittered with unshed tears. "I can't believe any of this happened."

"I know. Me either." Fresh sorrow hit her, and she motioned for her friend to join her. Together, they sat on the edge of the exam table and leaned into each other as their tears fell freely.

The EMTs had managed to keep Joel alive until he was brought to the hospital, but he died before they could get him into surgery.

Maybe Sedona shouldn't feel sad after all he did to her, but he'd been her friend for so much longer than that. She was mourning the loss of the friend she thought she knew, even if it was as much his memory as the person himself. Had he always hidden those kinds of feelings and anger, or was it a newer development? Sadly, they'd never know.

The door opened, and the nurse came in with a gentle smile and several pieces of paper. "You're good to go, Ms. Reeves. There are care instructions here. If you have any concerns, you should make an appointment with your primary care physician this week."

"Thank you." She accepted the paperwork and hopped off the bed with a flinch. Her head was still throbbing. "Can I please see Mac Durham?"

"Yes, but we'd prefer only one visitor at a time." The nurse told her which treatment room he was in.

"It's okay." Chloe reached over and gave Sedona a hug. "The others are out in the waiting room. I'll go give them an update, and we'll wait for you guys there."

Sedona followed the nurse down a hallway to another treatment room. When she pulled back the curtains and spotted Mac perched on the exam table, a wave of relief swept over her, washing away the heavy anxiety that had clung to her since they'd been separated after arriving at the hospital.

He got to his feet, and they met in the middle of the room. She sank into his arms and relished the warmth as they embraced in silence.

Mac leaned back to study her face, sympathy in his expression. "How are you feeling?"

"Sore. Tired. Like, bone weary." Sedona placed a hand on his arm just below the bandage. "How about you? Did you need stitches?"

"Four. It'll heal quickly, though. I told you, the bullet just grazed me."

They shared an unspoken acknowledgment of how close they both came to losing their lives tonight.

Mac swept some of her hair away from her face and lovingly tucked it behind her ear. "Any news about Joel?"

"He didn't make it." Her voice caught. "They tried, but he'd lost too much blood."

"I'm so sorry, Sedona. I know he was your friend."

"He was. But I guess I didn't really know him as well as I thought."

"I never should've left you back at the hotel. If I'd stayed…"

"No. It's not on you, Mac. I hope neither you nor Connor blames yourselves for anything because only Joel is responsible for what happened tonight." She reached up and placed a hand on his cheek. "I have no doubt that, if it hadn't been for you two, I wouldn't be here right now."

He reached for her hand and kissed her knuckles. "That you were able to maintain the presence of mind to send me the room number was a big turning point. I'm proud of you, Sunshine, and so very thankful that you're okay."

A local police officer came into the exam room and asked them both an exhausting number of questions and recorded their statements.

They were asked to go to the police station the following day, but for now, they were finally free to leave. Provided they stayed in San Antonio until the case was wrapped up. It was a relief when the nurse brought in Mac's discharge papers.

He took a double look at the printout. "Wow, it really is Wednesday, isn't it?"

"Really?" Sedona looked at the clock on the wall. "Can I just say, yesterday was one of the longest days of my life."

"Amen." Mac held out a hand, palm up. "You ready to get out of here?"

"So ready." She slipped her hand in his.

THIRTY

Even though Sedona was reluctant to do so, it was a good thing she and Chloe decided to postpone their concert in Dallas. Lou was going to work his magic to convince the venue to move it to the Saturday before Christmas, giving Sedona a week and a half to heal and the band time to find someone else to play bass for their last concert of the tour. Mac prayed it would work out.

It also meant less stress since it looked like it was going to take most of Wednesday to finish tying up loose ends in San Antonio.

Once they were discharged from the hospital, they all went back to the hotel. Mac wasn't keen on staying there after everything that happened, mostly because he was worried Sedona might not be able to sleep.

It was after nine in the morning now, and he still hadn't heard a peep from her. Hopefully, that meant she was resting well.

He glanced at the connecting door and smiled.

He'd already had phone calls from his parents and was now on the phone with Cole.

"Mom's worried about you. Are you sure you don't want

one of us to come down, pick you up, and bring you back to Destiny?" There was no missing the teasing in his voice. Cole knew full well Mac planned to ride with Sedona and her group to Dallas.

They'd already arranged for Cole and Asher to caravan to Dallas tomorrow, leave Mac's truck, and drive back to Destiny in Cole's.

As for Mac, he took a few days off work and intended to spend them in Dallas. Once Lou knew for sure when the last concert would be, Mac would adjust his own schedule as needed. He planned to be there no matter what.

He chuckled. "I'm good. It took a while to convince Mom of that, though. After you got shot in the shoulder last year, she was picturing worse."

"Well, thank God it wasn't. How's Sedona doing after everything?"

"Honestly? Emotionally, I'm not sure. I'll know more once I've talked to her today. Finding out it was her friend all along wasn't just jarring, but there had to be a level of betrayal there. Physically, I imagine she'll be sore for a while. It looked like her face was going to be pretty bruised up."

An image of Sedona being held at gunpoint, her face bleeding, flashed in his mind. It was one he wouldn't forget for a very long time, even though he'd like to.

There were so many ways it could've gone bad. He'd spent a great deal of time praying and thanking God that it hadn't.

Cole's voice brought Mac out of his thoughts. "Hey, I've got to run, but I almost forgot to tell you. Truitt accepted the job, so he'll be starting on Monday."

Mac grinned. "That's great. I'm glad to hear it."

"You'll be hearing from Asher shortly. He's been on the phone with Logan at the station nearly non-stop this morning. Tell Sedona I said hello, and you guys take it easy today."

"Will do. Give Erica and Peter my love."

They hung up, and Mac leaned back in his chair and turned the TV on.

It was nearly ten when a light knock sounded at the connecting door.

Mac switched off the TV and strode over to the door and opened it to find Sedona standing there, her smile lighting up the room, which instantly brought warmth to his heart.

"Good morning, Sunshine. Were you able to get some rest?"

"I barely remember lying down." She covered a yawn.

"Well, you obviously needed it." He wrapped his arms around her and gave her a gentle hug before leaning back again to look at her face. There was bruising on her cheekbone, and the stitched cut on her lip looked sore, but he was relieved that she didn't end up with a black eye. "How're you feeling?"

Sedona gingerly touched her face. "Not as bad as I thought I might. I think the worst is the cut inside my mouth. At least the visual stuff I can hide with makeup before we head to Dallas. I just figured the police may need an updated picture, or I already would have."

They had an appointment at the police station at one for some follow-up questions. Mac was hoping he'd be able to get his handgun back at that point and knew Connor was hoping the same.

"It's a good idea to wait. Are you going to be up for lunch?" They were meeting Connor, Chloe, Nick, and Lou in an hour.

"Definitely. I'm starving. How's your arm?" She placed a palm on his bicep just below the wound.

"It's sore, but I'll live." He smiled and leaned down for a light kiss, being careful not to touch the injured area of her lip. He was already looking forward to thoroughly kissing her again once it'd healed.

His phone pinged from its spot on the table. Mac took

Sedona's hand and brought her with him to see who it was. Asher's name flashed on the screen with a text. "He wants to talk to us on FaceTime. Hold on, let me grab my iPad."

Mac pulled a chair out for Sedona to sit and then moved the other close to hers before taking it. He turned on the iPad and forgot about the sketch he'd been working on. He hadn't intended to show it to Sedona before it was finished, but it was too late now.

She gasped. "Did you draw that?"

He shrugged. "It's not done yet." He'd been working on an image of Sedona sitting on a plush chair during one of her concerts, her guitar in her lap, and such a look of peace on her face. "It doesn't do you justice."

"Are you kidding? This is amazing." She leaned her head against his shoulder, and he kissed her forehead.

A FaceTime call came in then. He answered and set the iPad up on the table so they could both see it.

"Hey, man. How's it going?"

"It's been a busy morning so far. Good to see you both. Sedona, I'm sorry to hear about Joel and how everything played out. We're all praying for you here."

"I appreciate that." Sedona crossed her arms on the table-top. "I think I'm still in a state of shock, honestly."

"That's to be expected, I'm sure. It's a lot to process on multiple levels. How are you guys feeling?"

They gave him a quick update. "All in all, a whole lot better than we were not quite twelve hours ago," Mac finished.

"No joke. Well, we're all relieved to know you're okay. Mom would've been in the car at two this morning if Dad hadn't talked her down."

Mac chuckled. "I have no doubt about it." She was the mothering type, and even though he was determined to stay in Dallas through the weekend, he'd promised her he'd be home late Sunday night. "Cole mentioned you spoke with Logan this morning."

"Logan and Officer Carrington both. So, Carrington got that warrant in and confiscated the video from the gas station convenience store. Logan went through it and came back with a positive identification for the man who bought the burner phones. I'm sending a photo to you now."

Mac picked up his phone, waited for the text to come in, and pulled up the photo. As soon as it came on screen, there was no denying it was Joel. "That's definitely him."

Sedona leaned back in the chair away from the phone and shook her head. "I just don't understand why any of this happened. And the sad thing is, we'll probably never know now."

The sorrow in her voice triggered a deep ache in Mac's chest. He wished for all the world that she hadn't had to go through this.

"He must've hired someone to help with the delivery of some of those notes, plus the envelope you got at the concert in Destiny," Asher said. "Most likely, he found someone in the area and then handed them money and a set of instructions. Whoever delivered them probably had no idea what they were—everything else he could've done himself, including hijacking the IEM. A recording could've been made and set up to broadcast at a certain time. His actions were calculated."

"It may have been a mental illness that went undiagnosed and untreated over a long period of time," Mac told her. "You need to remember that none of this was your fault. There's no way you could've known."

"I know you're right. I just wish he had gotten the help that he needed if that were the case. I wish he'd said something to someone. Anyone." Her shoulders dropped.

"I imagine the investigation will continue for a while," Asher added. "However, I believe the police department in

San Antonio is heading that up. Officer Carrington said he'll make sure they get everything he has."

"We appreciate it, Asher. I'll be sure to send Carrington a text thanking him as well."

Sedona leaned forward again. "Yes, thank you so much for everything you've done."

Asher gave them a nod. "I'll talk to you later, Mac. And Sedona? Take it easy and feel better soon."

The video ended, and Mac closed the iPad.

He slipped his good arm around her shoulders and drew her close.

"Will you be okay?"

"Eventually. Thanks in big part to you."

THIRTY-ONE

TEN DAYS LATER

W hen Sedona made the decision to postpone the final concert, she'd second-guessed herself multiple times. It all worked out, though. Lou was able to convince the venue to move it back to the Saturday before Christmas. Through connections and friends, they found someone to play bass temporarily.

They also had a difficult conversation with Nick and let him go. He'd apologized for his behavior toward Chloe in San Antonio and accepted his fate with dignity. Another temporary musician was found to play drums. Once they got into the new year, they'd begin their search for new permanent members for the band.

Postponing the concert also gave Sedona's mouth a chance to heal. The cut on her lip was barely visible now.

In the end, it was one of the most memorable concerts Sedona had ever been a part of. Even though she and Chloe felt Joel's absence keenly, there was a peace that settled over the entire amphitheater. The audience seemed to love her new songs at the beginning of the night and joined in with the Christmas carol sing-along at the end. She'd finished the concert with tears in her eyes and a heart overflowing with gratitude.

They had enough special guests that they rented a large room at a local restaurant for an after-party so everyone would have a chance to visit. With food and time for conversation, it'd been a neat way to end the day and celebrate the holidays together.

Now it was getting late, and people were preparing to leave.

Sedona walked up and gave Connor a side hug. "I can't thank you enough for all you did during the tour. I'm so glad you and Jill could be here tonight."

The couple had driven up for the concert and planned to head home again in the morning.

Connor acknowledged her compliment with a soft nod and a warm smile. "Next time you're in Houston, I hope you'll stop by and say hello."

Jill walked up then and put an arm around her husband. "Yes, please. You're welcome at our home anytime."

"I appreciate that." Sedona gave her a hug, too.

The couple said goodbye to everyone else and headed out.

Mac walked up with Asher and Livi. It'd been fun to spend some time at dinner last night and get to know them better. It was too bad the rest of the family couldn't make it, though. Sedona had a feeling that seeing the whole family together would be an interesting experience.

She listened as the brothers laughed and teased each other about something.

Livi rolled her eyes. "They're always like this," she told Sedona.

"Sounds like fun," she said with a laugh.

"It is," Livi conceded. "Most of the time. Thanks so much for the chance to watch the concert and hang out with you this evening. It's been a lot of fun."

"Are you kidding? I probably wouldn't be here if it

weren't for you all. Thanks for everything you guys did." She reached out to give Livi a hug. "I'd really like to stay in touch. Would it be okay if I called or texted occasionally?"

Livi grinned. "Are you kidding? I'd love that."

Sedona turned to Asher. "I hope you guys have a safe trip home tomorrow."

"Thank you, we will. I have a feeling I'll be seeing you again soon." Asher gave Mac a less-than-subtle wink.

Not only did Mac not object, but he put a protective arm around Sedona's shoulders and drew her to his side. She was quickly discovering it was one of her favorite places to be.

"I'll be back in a few minutes." He pressed a kiss to her temple. "I'm going to walk them out."

"Okay."

Someone came up and nudged Sedona's arm. She turned to find Chloe holding a plate with a piece of cake. "Come on, you have to have one more with me. That way I don't look like a pig."

Sedona took it but gave her friend a dubious look. "Then we can look like pigs together?"

"Exactly."

They laughed as they made their way to where Grandma was visiting with Lou. Sedona couldn't get over how sweet he was, considering Grandma never stopped telling stories about "the old days." Apparently, Lou didn't mind.

Both musicians who'd helped them tonight stuck around just long enough to get something to eat and headed out a while ago.

"Did you want anything else to eat, Grandma?"

She patted her perfectly styled gray hair. "Oh goodness, no. Are you sure you and Mac don't mind taking me home? I could always call an Uber." As if she took an Uber all the time.

Sedona had to work to cover her laugh. "Are you kidding?

We're happy to. I'm just so glad you could be here tonight. It meant a lot."

"It meant a lot to me, too, sweetheart." Grandma patted her uninjured cheek. "I'm not sure I'll ever get over the shock of seeing your parents come into that amphitheater."

"I'm not sure I will, either."

Sedona had to take a second look when they took seats right up front. Mom hugged her and said she was glad she'd found her path. Dad shook Mac's hand and Connor's and thanked them both for their part in keeping Sedona safe.

It'd been the most effort they'd put into being involved in her life in a while, and she decided to accept the gift and be grateful they could be there for such a special night. Even though she invited them to come to the after-party, they declined. But they did comment on wanting to come back and see her for Christmas.

"I can't believe Christmas is less than five days away," Lou said with a shake of his head.

"It'll be the end of the year before we know it," Chloe agreed.

"I think we're all about ready to head out now." Sedona looked over her shoulder to see Mac coming back into the room. "If I don't see you guys before, I hope you both have a wonderful Christmas."

There were hugs all around.

Half an hour later, Mac and Sedona had taken Grandma home and made sure she got inside okay. Only then did Mac reach over the console for her hand.

"Are you up for a surprise?"

Her brows lifted. "What kind of surprise?"

He laughed. "No hints. And if you're too tired and need to go home and get some rest, it's not a problem."

"Yes, I'm up for a surprise."

Sedona tried to guess where they were going, but it wasn't

until he turned into a neighborhood that she realized what he had planned.

Known throughout the area for its extravagant holiday displays, the neighborhood welcomed guests to either drive or walk by and marvel at the Christmas lights.

He found a spot to park and turned to face her. "I know we never got the chance to check out the lights along the River Walk, but I thought this might be a good substitute."

Sedona's heart soared in response to his thoughtful gesture.

Without a word, she leaned forward and kissed his cheek. "This is perfect."

Grinning, he got out of the truck and circled around to help her out. Hand-in-hand, they wandered through the neighborhood, taking in the elaborate displays. Some of them were funny and especially creative, but her favorite was the beautiful recreation of the nativity, complete with lit palm trees and a lovely angel looking over the stable.

They were walking back to the truck when Mac stopped and gently tugged on Sedona's hand until she faced him.

"You know," he began softly, "I was thinking we could start a new tradition. Maybe bring some hot chocolate to sip next year."

"Next year, huh? Planning ahead?"

"You bet I am." He closed the gap between them and pulled her close. "I like the idea of starting some new traditions—especially if they involve spending time with you. What do you think?"

She stood on her tiptoes and gently touched her lips to his. "How about a Christmas movie tomorrow night? With popcorn? Or we could make some Christmas cookies."

He laughed and tenderly brushed a strand of hair from her face. "Is that a yes to new traditions?"

"With you? Always."

SPECIAL THANKS

I want to thank all of you wonderful readers for joining me on this journey as we dive into a new series. This book was so much fun to write, and I hope you all enjoyed getting to know Mac and Sedona as much as I did.

Steph and Alice, as always, you are both amazing at catching those pesky typos that manage to slip through the cracks. I appreciate you ladies.

Erynn, thanks for taking the time to go through my book with a fine-toothed comb and helping to make it the best it can be.

Doug, I couldn't do this if it weren't for your support. Thanks for always believing in me.

Sydney, I always enjoy sitting down and brainstorming with you, my girl. Thank you!

Most of all, I'm thankful to God for the opportunity to do what I love. To Him be the glory!

ABOUT THE AUTHOR

Melanie D. Snitker is a *USA Today* bestselling author who writes inspirational romance and romantic suspense. She and her husband live in Texas with their two children. They share their home with four dogs and two terrariums filled with a toad and two frogs. In her spare time, Melanie enjoys photography, reading, training her dog, playing computer games, and hanging out with family and friends.

https://www.melaniedsnitker.com/

BOOKS BY MELANIE D. SNITKER

BOOKS BY MELANIE D. SNITKER

Love's Compass Complete Series

Finding Peace

Finding Hope

Finding Courage

Finding Faith

Finding Joy

Finding Grace

Love Unexpected Complete Series

Safe In His Arms

Someone to Trust

Starting Anew

Healing Hearts

Calming the Storm

I Still Do

Don't Kiss Me Goodbye

Sage Valley Ranch

Charmed by the Daring Cowboy

Welcome to Romance

Fall Into Romance

A Merry Miracle in Romance

Made in the USA
Columbia, SC
02 November 2025

72558418R00132